Last Resort
By Alexander Cousins

Published July , 2015

This is a work of fiction. Names, characters, locations and events have been invented by the author or used fictitiously. Any resemblance to actual persons living or dead, historical events, or locations is coincidental.

Cover design and illustration by Julie Dillon

ISBN-13: 978-0994838407
ISBN-10: 0994838409

www.alexcousins.com

"We focused for so long on the dystopia of governmental control that we ignored the dystopia of unrestricted free organization. Our nobility now own corporations, not serfs."

—— UN Secretary General Silvia Flores, date unknown.

"Heroes are made either by their morals or by their success. The two factors rarely coincide."

—— Unknown

Origin

"Why?" Sybil Ferris asked, fists clenched.

"I can't do this. I refuse to be like father. I refuse to be part of the problem," Isa Ferris replied.

Isa faced her sister in a cherry wood hall gilded in platinum and gold. Servants parted around the pair, carrying about their menial tasks with downturned faces. Isa's trembling fingers clutched at a roll of crisp parchment that signed away her inheritance of Ferris Freight.

"What problem?" Sybil stuck a finger in Isa's chest. "Why choose *poverty?"*

Isa brushed her sister's hand away. She looks nothing like the little sister that snuck into my tutoring sessions, *Isa thought.* She's been recarved by the sculptor's knife. She looks like one of them. *"Our family wastes more money than the Ethics Commission has in its entire budget. I can have wealth but I'd have no purpose. I'd be rich and irrelevant."*

"You're naive. Wealth is never *irrelevant, and rejecting your birthright cannot change that."*

"I have to try!" Isa's voice boomed, sending a pair of servants scuttling out of the hall. "This world is flat fucking wrong, and I won't live in it."

Sybil's surgically perfected lips curled in a smirk. "You're wrong, but you're predictable. You'll see that I'm right, before the end."

"Fuck you." Isa unfurled the parchment and shoved it into her sister's chest. "I don't give a shit about your adolescent wisdom. I came here for your signature. Father won't let me leave until he knows that you've agreed to take the company on. Its medieval, but I need your help on this."

Sybil plucked the paper from Isa's fingers, and snapped for a servant to bring a pen. "Father does love tradition. I'll help you," Sybil said, pushing another servant down to his knees to form a table. The pen arrived and Sybil scratched ink onto paper.

"It's yours now," Isa said, sucking in a long breath.

Sybil stared at Isa, and straightened with parchment in hand. "I will give you a parting gift, Isa. You are dispossessed of the name Ferris. You will renounce all claim to the power and influence it holds. You will never use it to accomplish your goals. If you truly believe that this family's existence is unjust, then you will not benefit from it. You will become common."

"How is that a gift?"

"In return for this promise, I will not interfere in your idiocy. I will let you play at justice. I give you freedom, Isa; may it prove fruitful, even though we both know it will not."

Isa swallowed. "Fair."

Sybil nodded, and waved another servant over. "I have one more gift for you, before you leave." Sybil turned, holding a lacquered wooden box. She flipped it open, revealing a long revolver polished to a mirror-sheen. The perfect reflection was interrupted by the words Last Resort etched into the barrel. Isa saw the stress that tugged at her features in the weapon, and the steel in her gaze. She reached into the box and grasped the hilt. The weapon fit flawlessly into her fingers.

"It's perfect," Isa said.

"Of course it is," Sybil replied with a smile, the first real smile Isa had seen on her sister in months. "I wouldn't settle for less."

"Thank you, Sybil," Isa said, tears misting in her eyes.

"Go," Sybil replied, "this is no place for you."

***

Isa Ferris gripped a warm ceramic mug with shaky fingers as she dreamed of the past. She sipped coffee as she sifted through photos and documents on a data-slate with her free hand. Isa's room was more cell than apartment, its bed hunched against the same dull gray wall that held the griddle and a rack of utilitarian clothes. Flickering yellow emitted from a single bulb in the center of the ceiling, illuminating the desk and a large, and thankfully still secure, comms suite.

She gazed up at the buzzing stream of acquisition reports on her data-slate: *Dester Drydocks acquired by VDI (Void Defense*

Initiative) at 130.712% of market price ... Gussulle Naval Fabrication acquired by VDI at 117.263% of market price ... Edgely Stellar Hospital acquired by VDI at 176.208% of market price ... She bit a nail. *Void Defense Initiative? Never heard of them,* she thought, flipping through the company profile. *Where did they get the capital for so many buyouts?* The screen buzzed softly with more purchases. VDI blinked twice more on the display.

She flicked open a comms line. "Tibor. Some new front has been hitting the markets aggressively; check the known links between it and any major Multi-Planetary Corp." Her voice was frayed with fatigue. She ran a hand through disheveled strands of jet hair. Knots tugged at her scalp as her fingers passed through them.

"Morning, Ferris. Business first, as always." His voice growled slightly, the tone deep and resonant. "VDI has no known associations, but your family company is in that market. Tried talking to your sister?" A smile broke Isa's lips before she spoke.

"I'm not blind. Unlike you, I don't just look at vid-screens," Isa replied. They both chuckled before she continued. *He's getting the better of me these days.* Isa sighed inwardly. "This is too small-time for her. She is many things, but petty is not one of them."

"True," he replied. "I'll start digging. Dress corporate. I'll have a lead by the time you arrive."

"Confident," she mused.

"It's a win-win for me. Either you're prepared, or I get to look at you in a dress for the rest of the day."

"I have no idea why you can't find lasting relationships," Isa replied. "You're the perfect gentleman."

"My charm is legendary," the man replied. Isa could see his snide grin as he spoke. "Solenski has a transport waiting."

She flicked off the link, and moved over to her clothes rack. A chime brought her gaze down to her data-slate.

– Transfer missing from Ethics Commission wage service. Four pending transactions can no longer be completed. –

"Shit."

She pulled on a dress blouse with a neckline that plunged through vibrant oranges and blues. She hung a weathered leather holster over her shoulder. An ornate revolver, the only gift from her sister she had ever kept, glinted anxiously as she grabbed a box of fléchette rounds from the pocket of a simple gray coat. The pistol was stupidly antiquated, but it was reliable, and it was intimidating. Isa found both qualities endearing. She pulled on a pair of utilitarian black pants, and stowed the shells in a pocket before glancing at the comms suite and sighing.

She knelt beside the machine, and scratched at the hard drive with gnawed fingernails. The part popped free. She threw it on the ground and loaded the revolver, revealing the words Last Resort etched on the barrel. She stooped and slammed the pistol butt-first into the hard drive, obliterating plastic and silicon. She grunted, and hauled a leather bag from her nightstand, picking up a thin black coat before stalking out the door.

She left the cracked concrete hallways of her complex to a chorus of wailing infants and yapping dogs. A drab slate-gray transporter hummed in wait for her, paint scratched away in an uneven rectangle where they had removed the Ethics Commission logo three years ago after they found the microchips in the paint that alerted every major Multi-Planetary Corp office before they got there. The door slid upward, revealing Alain Solenski behind the wheel.

"What took you so long?" he asked, grinning through pale scars that ruined his face and left gaps in his tan beard. "Carefully applying makeup again?"

"Funny. Check your accounts? You might put lead in your walls if you read what I just did." The man's grin died.

"Again."

"What do you think, Solenski? Destroy your hard drive. We now have the pleasure of working from a home-office."

"Fucking government. Useless shitbag of an institution," he said as he pulled into traffic. "At least Terrestrial Security Syndicate paid me. Before Guardian Defense Corp bought it, and forced me into *this* job."

"Fucking corporations," Isa replied, "Setting up off-world accounts and using barely disguised fronts to conduct business to avoid taxes."

He glanced at her, his scars resisting his frown.

"You're a Ferris. You're a member of the corporate nobility. Can you really complain about corporations?"

"I'm an Ethics Commission Interrogator, aren't I?"

"You're an idiot. You had Ferris Freight as your inheritance, and now you can't afford your apartment. Why did you piss on success?"

"I …" Isa paused, "I didn't want it," she replied.

Solenski laughed. "Not good enough. Did your sister force you out? What happened?"

"How many times have we had this conversation?" Isa asked coldly. Solenski grunted, and shook his head. *This is what it has come to. All we have left are idealists and unemployed mercs.*

"I'll keep asking the damned question until you give me a real answer."

"I've told you the real answer every time."

"You've told me a fucking lie every time. Your interrogation bluffs don't work on me." Silence stretched through Isa's glower until they halted in front of an ill-kept spire of glass and marble. The Ethics Commission office bordered on dilapidated. Rust stains wept from the corners of windows. The concrete steps that rose to meet the entrance were littered with broken chips of cement. Isa holstered Last Resort, and hid it under the folds off her coat. Solenski crawled from the vehicle beside her and trudged up the stairs.

The complex was almost vacant. The pair stepped past a desk that should have been occupied by a secretary and into a clutch of desks centered in the open floor. The elevator doors smiled drunkenly at them from across the room as they saw Tibor hunched low over a mass of screens, cables, and input nodes.

"Tibor," Isa called, "Check your accounts?"

"Again? Damn it. I was just getting used to regular pay and job security. Don't suppose you could ask your sister for funding?" Tibor stood, revealing close-cropped blond hair and a soft frame. A dull mag-rifle stood propped up against the wall, twin magnetic rails blackened.

It's a good prop. I'm sure he barely knows how to fire the thing. But, with canister rounds, you barely need to.

"I'll ask my sister for funds when you can beat me on the range with your damned rifle," Isa replied. Tibor glanced up at her with a grin.

"You wound my pride irreparably."

"I'll settle if your sister gives me a real job," Solenski offered.

"What do we have on VDI?" Isa asked, ignoring him.

"It's being backed by a number of hedge-funds that we have on the blacklists as known tax evaders. Nothing sticky yet, but the digital records are surprisingly *under maintenance.*"

Isa nodded.

"Keep digging. I doubt they have it hidden too deeply. Do you have an address?"

"Nothing official. Server locations are protected by proxy, which is standard fare."

"They must have a meeting site in the Fiscal City. Hedge-fund owners don't travel off-world."

"I hope you're right," Tibor replied, checking a large central display that occupied a wall. "The Periphery's untouchable. If they meet on Varcona or Ispus we might be able to catch them yet. We have nominal jurisdiction there, if it hasn't yet been contracted to GDC."

"Those are the only two worlds other than Earth with a reasonable time delay on communication, correct?" Isa rearranged her holster absently as she spoke.

"There's the Contract Zone. GDC has an information relay at Grimvaldi Prime. Syndicalist resistance has been particularly heavy there, so I doubt it will be a base, but it is away from our prying eyes."

"Grimvaldi is too risky," Isa said. "We can eliminate that from the list. The Water *Barons,*" she said, filling the word with derision, "are too obviously in support of the Syndicalists. They forget that calling yourself a baron doesn't change anything but what your servants call you."

"Are we going to *theorize* all day?" Solenski interrupted. "If you two want to talk bullshit, I'll try and fill my schedule for the day with manual labor. I might even get paid."

"Oh, don't worry, Solenski," Tibor said. "You're a charity case. We don't *actually* expect you to contribute. Just nod your head and shoot when you're told to."

"If I was an armchair academic, I might be offended by you. Since I need to eat, I'll take a paycheck over principle."

"We'll get back-pay," Isa shot at Solenski. She turned to Tibor, and softened. "He's right. We need to find someone who is involved with VDI. Can you work some data-magic and get me what I need?"

"Will do," Tibor replied.

"I'll sabotage my comms suite, and get Tibor's as well,"

Solenski said. "Don't worry, I won't shoot up the place, you'll get your damage deposit back."

"What a kind man," Tibor replied. Isa turned, and walked to the elevator, hand resting on Last Resort's handle. She thumbed the button labeled Basement – Shooting Range. The elevator doors shuddered slightly before returning to their usual grin.

Fools

Sybil's fingers danced gracefully along a host of control panels as she chose how to sculpt her body. She rotated a holographic mannequin and altered select features. She brushed a hint of olive into her skin, and paled her tawny hair to silver. She gently accentuated curves and raised cheekbones. When she finished, a needle hissed outwards. *Elegant, not lusty. These are the ball and banquet types. I must look like a matron.* She sunk the needle into the pale flesh of her arm, and fell backward into cushioned mechanical limbs. Her thoughts began to cloud almost instantly, but through her failing vision, she glimpsed a figure in sterile surgical white enter the small room, pulling a cart laden with instruments, fluids, and synthetic bone.

***

Sprays of color marked swirling dancers as they flowed from partner to partner across the mahogany expanse of White Hall. Sybil flashed smiles and dipped gracefully to expose her flesh as men spun her. She caught glimpses of blocky GDC battle-harness through the press of merrymakers. Her pulse quickened. She deflected two propositions and nine offers for joint ventures that were as pointless as they were quaint. The crowd pressed and recoiled in time with a hidden orchestra. Sybil danced with a host of peripheral pseudo-noteworthies before she found her goal.

Sybil's arm caught the hem of her target and pulled the woman close. She wore a gown of mirror silver that contrasted her ebony skin and jet hair. Sybil saw the arterial crimson of her own gown as the spins of their dance brought them close.

"Helen," Sybil said as the dance brought her to the other woman's ear, "You have brought the family grace to the Peripheral Worlds, as I would expect of the Matron of White."

"You are kind, Sybil," Helen returned. Her voice was husky and rich, and she knew it. "I miss the glamor of the Fiscal City. Is the wine as good as I remember?"

"Better." Sybil gave a smile. "One of the recently settled outer worlds has a fruit that makes exquisite wine. Visit me sometime; I have a permanent contract for a private reserve."

"A Ferris never can do without." Helen chuckled.

"Why did you leave?" Sybil asked as she pulled Helen out of the interlocking morass of revelry. She picked two glasses of champagne off a tray held by a crisp man in a crisp suit. Sybil's taster materialized from the throng, lifted the champagne to his modified retinas, and scanned. He gave a short nod, then disappeared again.

"We're old friends; why don't you trust the security of my hall?" Helen jerked a thumb in the direction of the retreating taster.

"I trust you, but I do not know all of your guests. Forgive my paranoia; the Fiscal City never tires of poisoning drinks." Helen gave a shrug, and Sybil continued. "Alloy Industrial suffered no dip that I saw."

Helen switched to the lead, and passed through one of many marble-encased arches into a hallway that must have been fourteen feet tall. Intricately carved cherry parted as Helen's sable hand turned a knob of inlaid gold. The door clunked shut solidly. A puff of lavender emitted from the fumigator.

"You always did share my tastes." Helen smiled, but it quickly faded. "Someone made a covert move. My extraction facilities on Ignus Minor were sabotaged on the same day as my mills on Nestor's Rest."

"The Syndicalists targeted every major family. I lost nine docking facilities in the same week."

"This was different. GDC patrols increased in your sectors, correct?"

"Not perfectly," Sybil admitted. "There was a run on GDC contracts. They couldn't meet all of their security commitments."

"I didn't get any additional vessels or dragoons. GDC was late by a month to protect my external holdings."

"Why did that necessitate moving to the Core's edge?" Sybil took a seat in a throne upholstered in the skin of some extinct animal. Helen took a seat beside her.

"Precedent." She ran a tired hand through her hair. "They can't fail to uphold my personal security curtain; it would lead to a disastrous drop in confidence. So I moved my curtain to enclose my most valuable factories. I can at least ensure their protection."

Sybil laid a hand on Helen's leg, gently giving her a comforting pat. "A bribe could have done the same. There was and is no need to risk yourself. Why did you leave?"

Helen turned and inhaled deeply. "Do you ever wonder why the Syndicalists rebelled? Do you think they hate us?"

Sybil had to school her visage forcibly. *Naive inheritance-wealth idiot. We have everything anyone could want. Power, money, sex. Nothing is outside of our reach. They pay for our decadence with every servile breath. Of course they hate us. But we have the power. They seek to take it from us, and we will see them exterminated for their desires.*

"I don't know," Sybil finally answered. *I need more than this. I need preferential pricing for her metals. Alloy Industrial isn't the largest supplier, but it's the one I can get.*

"I think they do," Helen said. "We give them work. We give them all the opportunities they have in their lives. How could they hate us?"

"All we can do is keep the family holdings strong. We can't concern ourselves with the Syndicalists when legacy is at stake."

"You're so strong. Alloy Industrial should have passed to my brother. He's more like you. He has steel in his bones."

"Don't be foolish," Sybil said softly. Her hand moved to rest on Helen's. "It's difficult. You inherited recently, and the adjustment is difficult. I lost for fourteen consecutive months before I gained. It happens to all of us, we're just too proud to admit it." Helen looked into Sybil's eyes with welling tears, and pulled her into an embrace. Sybil could smell her fragility. Her fingers began to tremble as they encircled the skin of Helen's exposed back. *So delicate. Ripe for the taking. If I don't do this, GDC will send someone who will.*

"You remind me of Isa. My sister has a heart made for another age."

"Your sister was always more principled," Helen said as she sniffed. "I have concerns and I do nothing. Isa sees wrong and sets it to right."

Sybil pulled back and ran a hand gently over the tears that streaked the other woman's cheek. Orchestral chords and chattering voices reverberated through the door. Helen seemed not to hear them.

"GDC betrayed you, Helen," Sybil whispered. "They betrayed all of us. We must make them face repercussions."

"How? I want to see them pay, but I can't. They have a monopoly on force; surely you understand how that makes them untouchable."

"They aren't anymore. Their reliance on human soldiery has put them at a comparative disadvantage with other prospective incorporated armament firms."

"You're thinking Darwin? Aren't they a GDC subsidiary?"

"GDC is attempting a hostile buyout, Darwin is resisting."

"Why are you telling me this? Why do you need me?"

"Alloy Industrial has a steady and reliable supply of various metal alloys. I have vast holdings in multiple dry-dock facilities, and several shipwright subsidiaries."

"You seek to challenge GDC in stellar combat? GDC's naval capacity is their largest and most used asset. You'll lose. Find another way. I don't want to see you dead." *How touching. You're a child Helen, and this is a world that exists for the strong to seize it.* Sybil nodded.

"Thank you. It's a risk, but I have reason to think it will be worth my while." *Logistical supercomputing banks can run code-breaking software as well. I will have the first strike. It must be such a blow as to shake investor confidence on impact. I doubt I will win any sort of protracted conflict.*

"That still doesn't explain why you need me," Helen replied.

"I need preferential pricing. I won't be able to produce the warships that my subsidiary has designed unless I can gain access to your metallurgical products."

"I trust you, but you're contradicting yourself. How can I be concerned about legacy, and throw away profit at the same time?"

"Is it better for your legacy to be static and fear upheaval, or to be part of the coalition that toppled GDC?"

"I can't risk my family's name." Tears spilled from flushed sockets.

Sybil repressed a triumphant grin. *You're mine now, you malleable excuse for a tycoon.* Tears slid down Sybil's own cheeks now, her modified ducts spilling on command.

"I know it's not easy. I can't bear to think that I could be the last Ferris." *If medical technology can make it so, I will be. Helen shouldn't worry. Being the last White means being the last of an insignificant collection of Peripherals,* Sybil thought as she glanced down in fake humility. "I'm sorry." Tears wiped away, she squared her shoulders. "It has to be done. We cannot wait and allow other families or our descendants to struggle against a problem we could solve. There is no surer way to eliminate our legacy than maintenance of the status quo. Upheaval is necessary."

"I will give you what I can," Helen said.

"That is all I can ask," Sybil responded, and rose, smoothing her dress. "I will see if I can find you alternative security solutions so you are not at the mercy of GDC." Sybil turned to leave, footsteps clicking on the hardwood floor.

Jurisdiction

A slight smile tugged at the corner of Isa's lip as she sat in the dull gray of the Ethics Commission transport. Solenski gazed absently in the driver's seat, mostly disinterested. Tibor, who had gotten this tip in a matter of hours, shared Isa's excitement. He drummed his fingers on the stock of his mag-rifle. Across a street polluted with shifting masses of suited and elegant business people, a bulky man in dress uniform followed a woman in crisp sapphire. They entered a squat building almost hidden by the shadow of two massive towers on either side.

"Was that an admiral's crest on his shoulder?" Tibor asked, sucking in a worried breath.

"I think it was," Isa said slowly, checking that Last Resort was loaded. "It's time to move. We'll intercept whoever meets with the admiral, and question them. I wish our last door-tap didn't break last month." She turned to Solenski, and the man was alert now, soldier's reflexes tensing. "Solenksi, you're with me. Tibor, bring the transport around and ensure we have a quick escape. I guarantee both of them have bodyguards dispersed in this crowd."

"Will do," Tibor replied. Solenski just grunted, and produced a four-foot length of steel. Isa raised an eyebrow.

"Null-blade," the man replied. "I'll stun if possible. If not, this thing can liquefy the nervous system."

"Showy."

"A fucking *revolver* with fléchette rounds isn't?"

"Fair point."

They moved through the crowd subtly, remaining just far enough away from each other that they weren't obviously working together. A beggar watched Isa too closely and too efficiently. The woman was too well-fed to fit the part under scrutiny. *But then again,* Isa thought, *beggars aren't under scrutiny.*

She slipped into the shadow that hid the squat building, and cut to a side door. She was almost invisible to the street now. The occasional splash of color marked a businesswoman in her peripheral vision. Solenski slid up next to her, his null-blade humming softly.

Voices echoed faintly from inside the building. *Shit, they don't respect us enough to think we would listen at a door?* Isa's smirk broadened.

"So you're offering to double my salary and give me strategic command?" A cultured male voice said. Isa labeled it as the admiral's.

"We are. In return, you provide us detailed and accurate information on GDC supply, tactics, and current deployments. We also need your assistance in infiltrating an e-security team to sabotage GDC communications." The woman's voice had a hint of huskiness, likely altered so that she would be disconcerting during negotiations.

"That's a significant amount of risk," the admiral replied.

"It is. You have a reputation for being a good judge of risk. You know that GDC is rotten. It's a dying institution that would have promoted you to overall naval commander if it had any sense."

"I will command fewer ships in your company. Competing with GDC can be … lethal."

"Lethal when you command the strike force. Who will GDC send to claim you? Vaska? He's too cautious to catch you. Erramun? Too reckless. You'll gut his fleet on first contact."

"They will send Sabah." The admiral's voice darkened noticeably.

"Wouldn't you enjoy that?" the woman replied. "We can let you humiliate her."

"Appealing to my anger? I thought that was beneath you."

The woman laughed. "Please, I know you don't have principles I could offend. We need you, Admiral. Without you this initiative will not succeed."

"I understand. Where would you strike to shake shareholder confidence?"

"The Thusis Shipyards."

Shit. Isa breathed. *Thusis produces a third of GDC vessels.*

"You'll have to strike fast. GDC controls naval travel almost exclusively. I give you eight months before GDC thinks VDI is a problem. Ten months, and fleets will be at your dry docks, seizing them for GDC use."

"We've been stockpiling for some time. We made our first obvious buy this morning."

"Ambitious."

"Necessary."

"Your chances of success seem negligible, even if you have stockpiled effectively. Nothing you have said has convinced me that you will succeed. I hold no loyalty to GDC, but neither do I wish to die."

"I can say little else other than what you know. GDC is waiting to die, and you can either perish in the flames or light the match."

"I'll ignore your posturing. Who's your benefactor?"

"I am not at liberty to disclose that information."

"Then I am not at liberty to command your fleet."

"I can say this much," The woman replied, "our benefactor is almost as old and entrenched as GDC itself. It commands significant resources."

"One of the families," the admiral whispered.

"Will you lead the VDI?" There was no answer for a long moment.

"I will," the admiral replied.

Isa drew back from the door. She waved Solenski aside, pushing him deeper into the shadows. She exited as inconspicuously as she could manage and melted into a loose blob of corporate staff. She signaled Tibor with the data-band that she held loosely around the cold sweat on her wrist. As she suspected, the admiral exited first. The man was cold and square featured. He nodded, and the beggar rose, looking as if she was trying to find a more comfortable place to beg. Isa switched directions and moved with the crowd for another long minute until the woman exited. Solenski drew up, null-blade glinting in the shadow. Isa stepped from the crowd, and drew her Ethics Commission writ from a pocket.

"Shit." The woman's husky tone made the word more sophisticated than it was.

"Interrogator Isa Ferris." The woman gasped slightly as Isa continued. "I have some questions for you."

***

Isa wore Last Resort openly on her hip. It glinted dangerously in the dirty yellow light. The revolver was light, missing the complement of fléchette rounds that she normally wore. She stared at the sapphire-clad woman with crisp gray eyes. *A loaded weapon voids the evidence of the interview on the grounds of coercion, but an empty weapon is just a prop.* The woman's immaculately styled blonde hair was interrupted with stray locks. Her hands rested still on a blank steel table, while she shifted uncomfortably on a blocky metal chair. Beside the woman a data-slate sat slightly crooked.

"Camilla Lundahl," Isa said. "You've been busy." Isa leaned on the table, and plucked a loose collection of papers from the folder. "Fourteen dry-dock facilities, three mobile hospitals, eight fusion power plants, four mining complexes, and twelve dedicated research and development firms." She gave an exaggerated flick with each new item. "That's an impressive five years. Interesting, it seems that you rely on venture capital but have produced only minimal revenue. How exactly do you maintain investor confidence?"

"My investors have full knowledge of my finances. What they see evidently gives them confidence."

"Confidence in what? I'm no corporate expert, but it would take an idiot to invest in the VDI. You have dry docks but no ships, research teams but no prototypes." Camilla gave no answer. *Not working. Intimidation is the best option.*

Isa slammed a fist on the table. The metal hummed, and Camilla jumped.

"I know you're a front," Isa snapped. "Do you think we're blind? I've personally investigated Fulman Capital for tax evasion. They're your primary benefactor, correct?"

Camilla looked at her flatly. "Fulman's head office is on Ipsus; they aren't technically under Ethics Commission jurisdiction. They're a foreign investor."

"Have you ever been to their head office? One employee. Their satellite in the Fiscal City has six hundred employees. Exactly how 'foreign' is Fulman Capital?"

"That doesn't concern me. Do you have charges, or will you imprison me without cause?"

"I can hold you for a few days as part of an interrogation. Meanwhile, we'll pull down all websites associated with your name for investigation. I imagine you will look far more risky than you did previously."

"You're not intimidating. I don't need public confidence. I'm not publicly traded."

Not working. Isa paused, looking thoughtful.

"I'm confused about one issue. Shipping companies need dry docks, fuel, and raw materials. But you also purchased mobile hospitals and a staggering amount of research capacity. Surely you weren't planning to challenge the GDC naval monopoly?"

"You're mistaken," Camilla said, her tone slightly too even to be natural.

"I hope I am. As far as I understand, the only way you could succeed is with the element of surprise. Now, I don't think GDC cares at all about your little firm. But GDC is generous with Ethics Commission agents who are free with information relevant to their interests." *A bluff. My best chance at getting better information now.* Camilla bit. Her fingers shook for an instant, belying her calm.

"What if I was cooperative?"

"I don't care about whatever you're planning. I want Fulman. Where do they meet?"

"They met last on Varcona. Once I leave here, I am to set up a meeting on Grimvaldi Prime."

Isa drew in a sharp breath. "Grimvaldi? It's a war zone."

"It won't be by the time the meeting occurs. My employer bribed GDC to end the conflict as soon as possible," Camilla said softly. *GDC does not bribe cheaply. What family can afford these buyouts and combat operations?*

"You will tell us the location and time of the Grimvaldi meeting. Then you will continue on whatever mad vendetta you have against GDC."

Isa stepped out of the interrogation room. Water dripped in regular intervals from a leaky ceiling pipe in the flickering light of the concrete hallway. Tibor caught Isa's arm as she shut the door.

"You recorded that?" Isa asked, knowing the answer already, but in this case wanting the confirmation anyway. Sweat clung to her scalp, and she raked a hand through her hair.

"What do you mean you don't care what she's planning?" Tibor said, his tone low and venomous. "This is civil fucking war. We have no *idea* where this leads."

"I don't think we could stop it if we wanted to. What laws cover this? It's legal for an incorporated army to conduct combat operations outside Earth's direct orbit, as long as noncombatants are left alone." She looked at the man, and shuddered slightly. "What could stop them if they wanted to fight on Earth? Us?"

"No one."

"This way, if we can claim Fulman's assets, we could use the promise of their money to hire GDC to take it. We could actually fund the Ethics Commission with that money."

"Not going to work. GDC will accept Fulman's counter bribe, and lose no dragoons."

"We have to try," Isa replied, pointing to the leaking pipe. "Look at us. Look at this. We can't even enforce on Earth where we *do* have jurisdiction. We're not even worthy of the title 'organization.' We're two idealist crusaders. Humanity moved on, but we have to try to make this right."

"You know I agree," Tibor replied faintly. "I'll fall on the sword alongside you, but you have to know that it isn't going to work."

"It will. We'll find a way. We have to."

"I admire your optimism." Tibor gave a small smile. "I'll have to learn to use that mag-rifle."

Isa returned a grin. "I'm sure Solenski would be happy to help."

"Fuck you, Isa." Tibor said without malice.

Chess

The Tactical Command Unit's display lit the amphitheater's basalt in a kaleidoscope of holographic battle data. Syndicalist formations blinked red, dull notations hovering over their positions to indicate their fighting strength, the status of their cover, and their estimated weapon output. The hills and forested valleys of the peripheral war-zone Demos IV were rendered frosty by the harsh blue grid-work of the tactical hologram. A crescent ridge dominated the northern topography, its crest covered in red symbols. Syndicalist Strongpoint – Ironback Pass hovered in amber above the deployment. Various armored forms lined the tiered semicircular seating above the display. Some were in the block ceramic and scale of the GDC battle-harness. Masked helms at their sides revealed shaved scalps and faces cleaved by scars. Other figures had features sculpted in the latest style, and crisp suits of neutral colors, or extravagant gowns of numberless fabrics and gems.

Patris Telby stood hunched over a command console at the end of the Tactical Command Unit, ignoring the excited hum of the onlookers and the clatter of servers as they sated the audience's desires. Trailing cables linked him to the table by the temples and data-meshed his cortex with the computing unit of the display. His focus flicked to his arrayed battle organisms as they loped toward enemy formations in flickering green. He borrowed the eyes of a Feline Quadruped in the pack he had sent to flank the enemy's ordinance on the ridge. Patris turned the beast's head, surveying the dozen clawed and scaled beasts as they leaped and maintained speed despite the scattered boulders on the hillside. *We have the right blend this time. The midnight stalker of Eligos has a superior muscular structure to Earth's cheetah.* With a thought, he returned to the overhead view, and the public display shifted with him. The color splash was distracting, but nothing Patris could not handle. After all, investors couldn't see the unfolding battle any other way.

He summoned a herd of two hundred and thirty-eight chitin-plated infantry bipeds. Their exoskeletons were pitted and scarred by the small-arms fire and shrapnel raining from the ridge. Sensory antennae flicked atop their crested skulls as they responded to his urging. Their back-jointed limbs propelled them forward as they brought their bone-shield arms up to cover their torsos. They kept close, locking shield arms and loping toward the enemy. As they closed to one hundred and fifty meters from the ridge, they lifted densely muscled and tubular weapon arms. Calcium carbonate barbs solidified as they hurtled through the air toward scrambling figures holding rifles they barely knew how to use.

At the corners of his vision, Patris watched his subordinates mingle with the gaping onlookers. Well-placed comments and prodding questions corralled the audience into Patris's display. He returned his focus to the performance. The Syndicalists buckled, their rifle rounds thudding harmlessly into the chitinous organisms. Higher caliber shells screeched and thudded into the bone shields of the bipeds, but even emplaced machine guns spat uselessly against the battle chitin. Scattered rocket fire detonated bipeds in the shield wall as their antitank warheads spat liquid metal into the innards of their victims. Patris shrugged off his borrowed senses and switched his focus to the heavy assault pack that was mobilizing on the foothills beyond the battlefield. Scattered conifers snapped against gargantuan shells as macro-tortoises snorted and strode over the milling bipeds at their feet. In a coordinated jolt, thirty-seven macro-tortoises and one thousand, three hundred and six bipeds broke into a run. The air was thick with pheromone secretions as the battle organisms formed into crisp ranks under Patris's direction. He sent them forward with a gentle prod.

He was flying now. His borrowed wings rode the air effortlessly. The avian scout wing soared high overhead, the tips of its feathers touched by frost. With a piercing gaze, Patris watched his creatures converging on the Syndicalist emplacement. Feline Quadrupeds dispatched rearguard soldiers with claw swipes, painting sandbags and earth with arterial spray. By now the reinforcements had reached the front line. Steam from the acid bile of the macro-tortoise billowed upward. He flipped to the eyes of a macro-tortoise just as it vomited into a rifle pit. Shrieks and singed flesh odor emanated from the clutch of Syndicalists caught in the deluge. Whistling barbs caught a Syndicalist officer as he attempted to claw away from the saturated emplacement. Jagged white spines pinned him to the ground and pulped his organs with their kinetic force. Cheers erupted from several onlookers as they voyeuristically indulged in the slaughter.

Detonations rocked Patris's focus. Tank shells burst the macro-tortoise he had been borrowing. Charred meat and shell shrapnel flattened nearby bipeds, slaying a few. Leaping to the avian scout again, Patris saw a column of treaded vehicles thundering along a back road west of Ironback Pass. Patris grinned. He hadn't expected armor. The vehicles were of different marks; some had guns set into their hulls, others had turrets traversing and locking onto macro-tortoise silhouettes. He prioritized those, sending pheromone signals to loitering avian assault organisms. Twelve split off from the flock of air support above the ridge. They flexed muscled haunches as they spread their impossible wingspans. They dove, their feathers howling as the air struggled to move through them. Specialized organ-batteries imbedded near the creature's ribs ejected membrane sacs as they snapped open their wings and pulled out of the dive. Corrosive fluid and digestive enzymes gummed the vehicles immediately. When the fluid poured through imperfect seals, the crews decomposed in their immobile steel coffins.

Cut off from support and pressed by bipeds and macro-tortoises from the front and mauled by Feline Quadrupeds from the rear, the Syndicalists broke. Companies dropped their rifles wholesale, and fled. They were slain nonetheless. Patris watched through an avian scout in disgust. The enemy had not thought to equip their soldiers with enough antitank armaments, and little to no anti-air missiles. Seventy-three battle organisms had been spent, and only one of those a macro-tortoise. The crowd applauded raucously, but Patris barely repressed a snort. The enemy commander had been infantile in his or her inexperience. The battle had not provided a challenge; it didn't even stave off boredom.

His mind was bisected as the neural connectors disconnected upon his victory. Bile crept into the back of his throat as the cognitive enhancement suite of the Tactical Command Unit left his control. His mind felt dull and fuzzy, like the memory of an amputated limb. His vision shuddered, and blacked for an instant. Blood rushed back into his skull. He had to master his stomach as he rose from his command throne. With a deep breath, he turned to address the audience.

"This has been a demonstration of Darwin Bio-Security's combat potential. This was a live combat, occurring on the galactic Periphery. This operation cost 12 percent less than standard, and achieved a thirty-seven point two-seven to one kill ratio as opposed to the industry standard of fourteen point three-eight to one. Best of all, our weapons are vat grown. There will be no recruitment fatigue, no search for volunteers to fill the ranks of Darwin. Our genetics are not mishaps." Patris stopped to catch his breath. "Darwin combat organisms are engineered for their scenario. Any battlefield condition will be assessed and conquered. No challenge is too large. No combat role is impossible. Thank you for your consideration."

Nods and covert whispers spread through the crowd as they stood. The assembly filed out slowly, catching last glimpses of holographic projections of combat organisms as they rotated above the Tactical Command Unit in crystal relief. Patris, noting the support staff moving into the amphitheater from service doors, took his leave. He took another look at the TCU as he left, and placed a weak hand against the smooth metal of the door

The sun cut behind Patris's eyes as he moved into the crisp morning air. A serving girl immediately approached him, selected by a GDC "talent" department, and altered surgically to what he found attractive in a woman. He did not turn, simply took the offered flask of iced water and moved on. *GDC can play games with the best of the fiscal elite,* Patris scoffed inwardly. *It does not mean I must play along.* For such an obvious ploy, it was troubling how effective it could be.

The patter of ceramic-shod feet brought Patris's eyes up. Two hulks marched in harness around a giggling woman in an emerald dress cut to showcase her obviously altered form. At her side, a chiseled man of the tall and dark trope clutched her slender hand. Patris suppressed a scowl.

"You're from Darwin, are you not?" the woman asked, wonder in her voice. "Darling, you will have to excuse us." She flicked a chestnut lock from her eyes of deep gray. Patris braced himself. *An inherited money type, that is certain. Her tastes are as shallow as they are obvious. I wonder how long she has worn that eye color, and had that body type? Let alone her hair. A child.*

"Leave us." She waved, sending the GDC guards into a bow and the man into a fabricated smile. She clutched Patris's arm and drew him back into the amphitheater with a small smile and a furtive glance to see if they were followed. Patris raised an eyebrow at how well the scan was conducted.

The door clanged shut, and she changed. She drew back her hands, and straightened into a regal stance. "Patris Telby," she said. The girlish tones drained from her voice. "I am Sybil Ferris. I saw your presentation, and was fascinated. Why is it that Darwin spends the least to kill the most Syndicalists and yet does not have operational command?" *Not a child then, a Ferris.* Patris mused, reevaluating.

Patris snorted, casting a glance at the TCU as an image of a macro-tortoise flickered at the edge of his vision. "GDC has the most robust navy of any private military corporation. They control trade lanes and police the bulk of the void. I have yet to see a viable spacefaring organism, or a plan for a dry dock that could grow one. Our combat organisms may be far superior to GDC dragoons, but we are unable to transport them without paying a tariff to transport craft."

"Have you attempted to use any other service?"

"No other service has the capacity required to transport an operational size herd and the alteration and birthing vats required to reinforce one. GDC is our only option," Patris responded.

Sybil's mouth curled in one corner. "So you're here at the GDC Expo to entertain their offer to buy Darwin Bio-Security. Allow me to counter offer. You keep your independence. I supply you with the capital that I'm sure you've guessed I have, and you create a valid force to compete with GDC. What price per share were you offered?"

"Three hundred thirteen per share. Our current price is three hundred ten. You will have to make the increase significant for me to consider offending the GDC Board of Directors," Patris replied.

Sybil raised an eyebrow. "Doesn't it anger you that you have to appease GDC? That you have to risk offending them?"

"Not enough for me to give you a discount," Patris said with a sly grin.

She returned the gesture. "I suspected as much. However,

Darwin is *too* effective. The Syndicalists are at best a minor threat to overall security. Darwin is not designed for that kind of engagement, especially considering your logistical … difficulties. You see, Patris, your share prices are inflated. No one *needs* the level of combat power Darwin supplies. However, you're new, and that makes you interesting."

"Why are you interested, then? Why do you need Darwin?" Patris asked.

"Irrelevant. I have money, and you resent the GDC monopoly. We can help each other," Sibyl replied.

"It's very relevant. GDC wants to buy me so that they can dismantle and absorb my tech. They wish to maintain their monopoly. Prove your motivation is better."

Sybil straightened. "I am a Ferris," she said. "We make our living by conveying water from the Baronies of the galactic Periphery to the waterless Corporate Worlds. GDC charges trade tariffs that are so crippling it would be more affordable to buy our own defense corps than pay them, so we're doing it."

Patris shook his head. "You're not very convincing. Give me three-twenty, and I'm still CEO."

"Three-fourteen. That's as high as I'll go."

"I'd refuse your offer because I know you're lying, but I hate GDC as much as you do," Patris said as he shook his head. "They're backward and inept. They do not see the weakness of the human form in battle. Did you know that they created a division of 'altered' soldiers once they heard of Darwin? The 22nd Foot. The idiots cling to our genetics as if they were sacrosanct. Our brain is the only useful adaptation we have for combat, and we can easily enslave organisms to a human mind. Despite this, they will ask me to enhance soldiers, not create the perfect combat force. I will not do it." Patris spat, feeling the buzz in his head subside a little. *Besides, it will mean a stop to fighting Syndicalists. They're no challenge. GDC on the other hand ...* He looked the sculpted woman straight in her eyes.

"I'll accept under one condition."

Sybil raised an eyebrow, but said nothing.

"I know you can't afford me," he continued. "Certainly not right now, and it's absolutely false that any contract, however exploitative, is more expensive than buying me out. However, this will be worth our while if we merge."

"Shared ownership? Not an option."

"Not exactly. We'll merge our capital and retain oversight on our own companies. Together, we will form a counterpoint to GDC. You already manufacture stellar craft, so Ferris Freight will supply the navy. I'll accelerate organism development and birthrate so I can provide terrestrial forces. Together, we usurp the GDC monopoly."

Dedication

Executor Sebastian Verde filled the creaking swivel chair he sat
in. A faint web of microfractures marred the data-slate desktop
where he flicked casually through pages of data. The room was
dim, the desk sapping the power from a bank of overhead lighting.
A robust fumigator puffed a faint scent of pine from the corner of
the room before switching off.

"You realize how dangerous this is," the man said, his voice a
little shrill from the information Isa had given him.

"I have to do this."

"I'm sure you think so. I don't want one of my few
Interrogators to be captured by pirates, or Syndicalists. I can't
afford ransom. Not to mention we only have one functional
spacecraft." Sebastian scratched at a frosted temple nervously.

"You know what that money could mean. A full *working* office.
Equipment. Personnel."

"You don't need to lecture me on the gains. It's a gamble at best
and lethal at worst. Your legal grounds are flimsy, and your
guarantee of GDC support is flimsier. I can't authorize this, the
risk is too great."

"What exactly is the Ethics Commission able to do in its current
capacity?"

"Give the illusion of the rule of law in the Fiscal City. Take
bribes from corporate executives to pay rent and wages. Almost
nothing."

"You don't find that unacceptable?" Isa replied, fingers
beginning to clench.

"It's reality. The fact that it offends me couldn't be less
relevant," Sebastian replied coldly.

"We have a chance to change that," Isa said, pushing the words through clenched teeth. "Some things are worth fighting for. Our society is despicable. We advertise people with dollar values. If you own nothing, you're worth nothing. The law applies selectively to those who can't afford to bribe the court system. Justice doesn't exist. I see a way out, and you're seriously asking me not to pursue it?"

"I don't understand why you're criticizing me for asking you not to kill yourself. That's what this mission is. Suicide. If you don't understand that, you're delusional."

"Some things are worth dying for!" Isa's voice reverberated in the cramped office. "If I risk my life for justice, it's a fair bargain."

"If you had a reasonable chance of success, I'd be inclined to give you what you want. You don't. You've said your piece. I appreciate this, Interrogator, but I will not allow it."

Isa breathed for a long time. Her fingers itched to make fists, to slam the table, to rage. *It won't work on Sebastian. He'll just be more convinced that I'm not thinking clearly,* Isa thought, as she stamped her anger down. *I only have one option left: bluff.*

"Executor," Isa began, her voice stiff with formality. "I hereby resign my position as Ethics Commission Interrogator, as I feel I am no longer able to uphold justice on Earth, as is my duty."

"Isa," Sebastian said, a pleading note in his voice.

"I will take any and all penalties necessary for an immediate dishonorable discharge. I will return my writ of service, and forsake the ability to reapply for the Ethics Commission in perpetuity." Isa drew the writ from her pocket, and set it softly on the table. Sebastian leveled a stare at her, and glanced uncomfortably at the writ. Isa pounced. She saluted, and turned her back on the Executor with a click of her heels.

"Stop."

Isa turned back to the man, seeing her writ in Sebastian's outstretched hand.

"I'm not sure if I admire you or pity you, but I can't stop you. I hope for both our sakes that you're successful. I'll wire what funds I can to your personal account. We need deniability, you understand." Isa plucked the writ from Sebastian's hand, and flashed a smile.

"I will do what I can for the Ethics Commission. Someone has to."

***

Isa leaned against the clutch of desks and computing equipment that formed the last functional piece of the office. Tibor was rifling through data beside her, condensing and packaging the required information onto a reinforced data-slate.

"That's where we are. It's Grimvaldi Prime or nothing."

Solenski looked at Isa, and laughed.

"I'm no Idealist. There's no bonus, and stupid risk. Not happening. I'll apply to GDC again, or I'll dig a fucking trench, but I won't die on a promise."

"Alain," Tibor said evenly. "I don't like you. In fact, I think you're more ape than man."

"And I've taken shits with more sense than you."

"But even you have to have some sense of honor. You can see that the system isn't fucking working," Tibor finished, ignoring Solenski's interruption.

"I don't see how my death will change that."

"Do you trust me?" Isa asked, standing straight.

Solenski shifted uncomfortably, and finally met her gaze.

"Anyone willing to give up what you did is two things: stupid and committed. I trust you think you're 'making a difference.' But I don't care. I don't want to die, and this only ends one way."

"I'm asking you to trust me this once. It's going to be dangerous. I'd be happier with you at my back. Tibor's a useless shot." Isa cracked a grin, and Tibor shrugged his agreement.

Solenski's eyes went wide, his gaze bouncing between the two of them.

"What the fuck is going on? Am I trying to argue sense into you two? You're the educated little shits: you know I'm not being a coward. This is actually crazy. You said they planned to bribe GDC and build a fleet at the same damned time. How many companies can afford that? Do you know what level of shitstorm this is going to bring down on our heads? We might die just for talking about this. We might be dead already. But I can absolutely guarantee that if we pursue this, no one even sees our bodies or remembers our names. That Camilla bitch probably already has 'pirates' waiting just outside orbit, loitering for an Ethics Commission signal." He stood dead still. When Isa and Tibor offered no reply, he grunted, and shook his head.

"You're committed to this, aren't you?"

"Yes." Isa and Tibor answered as one.

"I tried to fucking save you," Solenski muttered as he shouldered past Isa toward the door. "I don't know why, but I fucking did." The door slammed behind him.

Isa turned to Tibor. "You're ready to do this?"

"I'm not going to let you get all the credit. Besides, the two of us alone, on a ship"—he smirked—"for *weeks* … Judging by that I've got good odds, even if it's just desperation."

They shared a laugh, and Isa boxed the man's shoulder

Duty

Grimvaldi Prime's port stank of human poverty. Desiccated people ambled from menial task to menial task with grim-faced determination. The cold metal and pastel-painted buildings rested in a loose, stained circle surrounded by prefabricated warehouses. Tibor stepped from the Ethics Commission transport behind Isa, which dwarfed the buildings around it. Their skeleton crew looked only slightly better fed than the dockworkers.

"Damn," Tibor whispered, tucking a data-slate under his arm. "Is anyone really surprised that the Syndicalists rebel?"

"No," Isa agreed. She pushed through the workers, and checked Last Resort under her jacket. *We can stop this the right way if we succeed here. All of it.* She shook her head slightly as she thought. *Not all of this; that will never happen. But we can make it better.* The streets wound through vendors and dense crowds. Isa glanced back at Tibor, who was staring at a graying woman curled into a ball on the street. Boots jostled the woman roughly as the crowd parted reluctantly around her. She gave no reaction as a steel-toed boot broke her nose.

"She's dead." Isa pulled at the man, pointing further down the street. "We have to move."

"Right, you're right." Tibor shuddered slightly, and followed Isa. A compact mag-pistol bulged under his coat, but no one took enough time to notice.

They pushed through the last of the crowd to find a barrier of mirror-sheen steel guarded by two men in the scale-and-plate battle-harness of GDC dragoons. The dragoons held military grade mag-rifles in their plated fists, and towered over the milling crowd.

"Hold. Wait for identity scans before you pass into the Capital District," one dragoon growled.

"Concealed weapons?" said the other, pointing first at Tibor's obvious pistol, then at Last Resort. "Costs extra. Vilmos, concealed surcharge on the entrance fee." Vilmos tapped twice on a bulked data-slate, and nodded.

"Billing a corporate travel account?"

Isa shook her head, and held up her wrist, revealing a data-band. "Personal account."

Vilmos completed the transaction, and the other dragoon waved them in as he opened a previously hidden door.

"You're paid until nightfall. Don't cause trouble." They walked through the open gate into a breath of lightly perfumed air. Somehow the fumigators had managed to block out the stench from over the wall. Air scrubbers probed into the sky and purged the pollution from the air before it passed into the Capital District. Men and women strolled amiably in loose clumps, laughing and plucking glasses of champagne from circulating servants in crisp white garb. Each servant was an unnerving image of alabaster perfection. Isa waved away one servant who approached them, and struggled to find a nook or space that wasn't well lit and facing a window. She came up short.

"GDC will be tracking my data-band. We have to smash it."

"They will know exactly what we did when it stops responding."

"But they won't know where we went and what we saw. No other option." Isa plucked the data-band from her wrist. She dropped it to the granite paving stones and crushed it with a heel. "Time to move."

***

Isa sipped an exquisite espresso that had the perfect blend of cinnamon, nutmeg, and vanilla notes as she pretended to lean casually on the café wall and observe the passersby. Around them, pairs and groups of corporate types sat at café tables, eating artisan baking with their various coffees and teas. Two men in business casual talked quietly at the nearest table, matching the descriptions Isa had pried from Camilla. Tibor pretended to read financial news while he recorded the nearby conversation on his data-slate.

"We'll transfer the sum in stages, and label it under a separate hedge fund each time," the Fulman representative said in a low voice. "Two stages will be from other investment firms we are on good terms with. It will cost you, but it should confuse GDC accountants enough to buy you another month of obscurity."

"Have the appropriate bribes been allocated to avoid taxation?"

"Of course. We are running every transaction through the Fiscal City office, for your convenience. Meetings of this nature will no longer be necessary."

"Excellent," the other man replied. Isa assumed he was the VDI representative. "What of the other matter?"

"The Water Barons have been able to increase the Grimvaldi Prime and Demos IV Syndicalist resistance forces in size and improve their equipment with your donation. GDC has deployed their experimental augmented soldiers, the 22nd Dragoons, to clean up both campaigns. The 22nd should conclude Grimvaldi today, by whatever means necessary. GDC also subcontracted the assault on Ironback Pass to Darwin Bio-Security. They will be observing that closely. That may distract GDC, even after they trace Darwin's new venture capital back to your employer."

"Any more business that must be discussed in person?" the VDI representative asked, waving away a waitress.

"No. All else can be electronic, unless the situation changes." The two men stood, and exited the café. Isa breathed. Tibor tapped off the recording and glanced at her.

"They don't even talk around illegal activity. They know we can't hurt them." He broke into a smirk. "Not anymore."

"We need to get back to the Fiscal City. This is enough to nail Fulman down." Isa grimaced. "The fact that their overwhelming arrogance hasn't caught up to them yet is disturbing."

Tibor's reply was drowned in the blaring roar of engines as two multi-nacelled jet transports tore through the sky overhead.

"I pity those Syndicalists," Tibor said as he pushed off the café wall and began to walk. Isa followed, focused on the conversation they had just heard.

"The 22nd is here."

"Hence the pity. Where the 22nd steps, butchery abounds."

They cut back through the clean streets and exquisite boutiques to the exit of the Capital District. The door opened, and they were assaulted once more with the stink of unwashed bodies. The two door guards nodded, and tapped their exit on the data-slate. After the careless stroll of the corporate types in the Capital District, these crowds had a frantic aspect to them. In the distance, a phalanx of dragoons escorted a pair of notables through the press.

People shrank back from them, eyes white and staring at polished mag-rifles glinting in the sunlight. *The Fulman employee said 'by any means necessary.' The 22nd is notoriously brutal. Even these dragoons wouldn't hesitate to gun down any of these people if they became a problem. What is happening outside this city?*

"Tibor." Isa's voice was soft, but it began to boil as she spoke. "The Ethics Commission has jurisdiction over war crimes, regardless of location."

Tibor's head snapped around to meet her gaze. "That's impossible." He shook his head. "We've had a spectacular victory today, don't ruin it by risking this."

Isa grabbed the man's arm roughly, eliciting a flinch.

"Do you see these people?"

"This is not the time for emotion. I get that—"

"This isn't emotion," Isa hissed, her grip tightening. "This is duty. We've been playing at law in the Fiscal City all this time, pretending we are fighting for justice. All the while these people live little better than slaves." She let go, and gave a humorless laugh. "There *are* probably slaves somewhere in the corporate zone. We can't solve everything, but we have a clear and obvious duty here, and the jurisdiction to enforce it."

"It's an active war zone outside city limits," Tibor replied slowly.

"I didn't say that it would be easy, only necessary."

"You would risk what we just found for this?"

"If we don't uphold the law, it may as well not exist," Isa said with an edge in her voice.

Tibor recoiled and nodded. "Fine. I understand. I'll follow your lead."

Isa nodded sharply and turned.

"What are you doing?" Tibor grunted as he followed.

"What my sister specifically told me *not* to do." She stalked back to the dragoons that held the door. The men straightened, and the one she thought was Vilmos held out a warding hand.

"The entrance fee only covers one entrance and exit. I'll have to bill your account again."

"I don't care about this peripheral excuse for luxury, dragoon," Isa snapped. She pointed at the other dragoon, and snapped her fingers impatiently. "I was promised a meeting with the commanding officer of the 22nd GDC dragoons. He was not present at the meeting location. I don't accept rescheduling."

"Ma'am," Vilmos began cautiously, "I don't have any record of such a meeting. You'll have to accept rescheduling in this case, as Commandant Gabriel Theros is on mission. He's due to return in four hours."

"Syndicalists take the GDC's elite troops an entire afternoon to clean out? I doubt it. You will transport me to wherever Gabriel is, and you will provide me with *comfort* while we travel. Am I understood?"

"You don't appear on the records."

"Of course I don't!" Isa snapped. "Do a DNA test." She held out a finger. Vilmos hesitantly disconnected a stylus from his data-slate and pricked her finger. *I can't forfeit my DNA,* Isa thought, and put on an air of impatience. Tibor finally clued in, and matched her scowl.

"My apologies, Madame Ferris," Vilmos said through his helmet. "I will arrange transport immediately, and notify forward units for escort. Forgive me, but only Satyr armored personnel carriers are available for the journey. It will not be … comfortable."

"It better be comfortable enough, or I'll waste some of my time with a complaint." Isa glowered. "I'll have time to waste with the drive ahead."

Vilmos tossed his data-slate to the other man. "Hold the checkpoint while I escort Madame Ferris," he said. "This way." He gestured, and Isa and Tibor marched after him.

***

The Satyr's interior was *not* comfortable. Its interior was roomy enough to transport fire-teams of dragoons, but the seats were almost nonexistent, save for a series of safety belts that fit Vilmos perfectly, but looked comically large on Isa and Tibor. Isa gazed at Vilmos flatly, and held out her hand to Tibor. The man set his data-slate in her palm, and she shook her head as she pretended to file a report. They drove in a wash of white noise for almost an hour before their convoy stopped. The dull interior of the vehicle was bathed in harsh light as the rear hatch clanked open. Vilmos unlatched himself expertly, and moved over to assist Isa and Tibor. They followed him out of the vehicle, stooping as they walked.

The scent of burned meat assaulted Isa's nostrils as soon as she stepped from the Satyr. A pristine triple rank of hulking armored forms stood before them, their apparent parade belied by coatings of ash and ruddy-black splotches that looked too much like fried blood. Isa suppressed the urge to vomit. Tibor was not so successful. Vilmos was shorter than even the smallest of these men. He saluted, and backed away. Smoldering buildings belched black smoke into the air in the distance

"Which one of you is Gabriel?" Isa called, pushing her anger into her voice. One of the battle-harnessed men stepped forward, an oversized null-blade hissing in his fist.

"I am Commandant Gabriel Theros," the man said. The scorched blood that caked his armor flaked off gently as he moved. "I was not notified of a meeting. What do you need?"

Isa reached slowly into her pocket, withdrew her Ethics Commission writ, and held it up. The 22nd stood statuesque, though Isa noticed their fingers tightened on their weapons.

"I am Interrogator Isa Ferris. I hereby place you under arrest for the suspicion of war crimes, given grounds by the state of your armor, and by the authority of the Ethics Commission of Earth."

Gabriel laughed. It boomed with a disturbingly rich quality as he turned to Vilmos. "*Interrogator* Isa Ferris," Gabriel replied. "This was unexpected." Another man stepped up, sweeping his mag-rifle in Tibor's direction.

"Commandant." The man's voice was deep and gravelly.

"No, Argus. Not now," Gabriel replied. He reached up to his helmet, and pulled it off to reveal a strong face ruined by scars. "I will submit for interrogation. This combat operation is concluded."

***

Gabriel loomed even without the assistance of his battle-harness. His lieutenants had aided him in taking off the steel-ceramic composite, muttering to themselves all the while. Now he stared at Isa as the Satyr trundled back to the port, his inspection unbroken by difficult terrain. The shackles around his wrists seemed too small to be meaningful, though they would have looked imposing on a normal man. Gabriel still smelled faintly of seared meat. His death-musk nagged at Isa, keeping her stomach unsettled. They entered the city at the port proper this time, and when the Satyr opened, it revealed the Ethics Commission transport gunning its engines.

"You first, dragoon," Isa said, hand resting on Last Resort's handle. The man nodded, and she and Tibor ushered the man into the transport. The blackened steel corridors were a blur to her. Her fingers shook slightly as she led Gabriel into a containment cell. They shut the door and Isa breathed again.

"Coffee?" Tibor asked, his voice wavering slightly. Isa nodded, and followed the man to the bridge.

***

It was almost an hour before her nerves stopped flooding her veins with adrenaline. She ran a hand through her sweat-ruined hair as she sipped gratefully at the cup Tibor had brewed for her. Two crewmen navigated and piloted the ship in front of them, fingers flying over the myriad levers, sticks, and buttons as they sat in two consoles. Diffuse orange light lit the room well enough, but the light flickered ever so slightly.

"Are we armed?" Isa finally asked, leaning on the wall. Tibor joined her and shook his head.

"It's a civilian ship. A *cheap* civilian ship."

"I have to go in there soon." Tibor looked at her sharply.

"You don't have to do anything, Isa. The man is a monster. Let someone else waste their time. You'll get nothing from him."

"I have to try. While the surprise still clouds his mind."

"More than it clouds yours?"

"Damn it, I've done hundreds of interrogations. I can handle this. If I wait too long we look incompetent. I can't start on the defensive."

Tibor shook his head again.

"When it doesn't work, I'll let you cry on my shoulder while I try to do something useful, like back up the recording we have."

"When I prove you wrong," Isa retorted with a grin, "I'll let you bask in my glorious presence."

"What an honor, *Madame Ferris*." He laughed. Isa drew Last Resort, popped open the revolver and dumped the fléchette rounds into her palm.

"Hide that recording somewhere where only you can find it. Take these, I'm going to force a confession from a monster." She pushed the bullets into Tibor's hands as Tibor produced a data-slate buzzing with Gabriel's combat records. Her fingers were slick as she began reading, and she clanked out of the bridge toward the awaiting Commandant.

Needs

Scent coughed from the wall-mounted fumigator as Patris stifled a yawn. This one was discreet, concealed in an ornate light fixture out of direct view, but the glint of a small metal grill gave it away. The device struggled to cope with Patris's contempt for its function, and the competing perfume preferences of the others in the room. It settled on a hint of pine just thick enough for Patris to smell. Sybil glanced at him from across the expanse of carved and gilded rosewood that made up the table and chairs of the conference room. Her youthfully sculpted features gave only the hint of an arched eyebrow before she turned back to the man standing over her and Patris, with his steel and ceramic scaled fists clenched on the table.

"What is the function of this meeting, Telby?" the man shrouded in battle-harness asked through a voice amplifier. "You're ours, bought days ago."

"Darwin Bio-Security is not a subsidiary of GDC. Not yet." Patris gave a nod toward Sybil. "I have received a counter offer. Now you must bid."

At this, Sybil's eyebrow truly raised.

"GDC can outbid her. This negotiation is pointless"

"We are not in a war zone," Sybil said, injecting a sultry note that hinted at what could be done outside a war zone. "Sit, let us speak face-to-face."

The plated man turned his visor plate toward Sybil. "Get this idiot girl out of my office." Patris repressed a grin. *Take your identification tag off your armor. Who in the Fiscal City doesn't have modifications? Either you are an idiot for wishing anonymity, or a complete idiot for thinking battle-harness would intimidate me. Or her. Especially her.*

"She may bid as well." Patris made the words conciliatory, but watched them hit like projectiles. *Has GDC truly been monopolistic long enough to expect only sycophants?*

"Fine. Three-twenty per share," Konrad replied. "That price is generous enough for you to forget whatever *favors* she gave you."

"Not quite," Patris said, casting a glance at Sybil through the corner of his eye.

Konrad shifted.

"Darwin will be in direct competition with GDC for all requisite material to wage war, and for wars to wage. It would profit you more to be a part of GDC than against it, but you're free to make mistakes." Konrad straightened, never having sat down. A plated finger indicated the door before he turned in a whisper of servos.

"I'm pleased this could be worked through," Sybil said. "I hope we meet again." She bowed, allowing the cut of her garb to expose the curves of her sculpt. Patris simply nodded, feeling a buzz dull the back of his skull. The office's doors flexed gracefully to reveal the spiraling expanse of glass stairs that led to the High Commandant's office.

Patris and Sybil stepped down together on stairs that could fit many more, allowing the clinks of Sybil's heels to fill the silence. Competing clinks answered them as a woman, young and curved, rose past them, a tray of coffee in her arms.

A sleek black automated transport waited for them at the door, a point of calm in the press of suit and gown clad officials. Other sleek transports glittered in the artificial sunlight, and the Fiscal City ground through time, heedless of natural patterns. Sybil had the door open; her clinging jade velvet snickered as it slid along the seat when she moved into the vehicle. She wore hair of deep copper today, with a set of emerald eyes and a pale complexion. As always, she wore her breasts large as an adolescent dream, with skin smoothed to almost youth. *Her sculptor must be the best in the galaxy,* Patris mused. *I've never seen someone able to shift appearance so naturally and so fluidly. She was bronzed, with locks of jet, when we last met two days ago.* Patris stepped into the vehicle, and heard a blurt of static as the internal countermeasures suite swept him for bugs and found him clean.

"Well?" she asked, the sultry veneer lifting once they were alone. Somehow she managed to make her appearance commanding.

"The birthing vats are prepped, and ready for transport. Demos is currently an active GDC war zone. The 22nd are deployed there in full, as well as the 13th, the 5th, and the 6th Jager corps." Patris paused. "If my sources within GDC command can be believed, the fleet presence is minimal: a carrier, *Crimson Dawn,* and its support fleet of approximately five destroyers. It's enough to blockade Syndicalist forces, but not nearly enough to stop interstellar travel completely. What of your task?"

She returned his grin then, exposing pearlescent perfection in a flash. "Blueprints of most GDC vessels have been stolen by my e-security firm while we were 'talking' with Konrad. GDC's protocols are complacent. We are currently working on a corruption executable to destroy the combat AI systems. When I know the full extent of what is possible in the corruption, we will begin to plan accordingly. Development on viable EMP warheads has also begun at my weapons subsidiary. However, once ship production truly begins, I doubt I will have the funds to cover both R & D and vessel production. I'm sacrificing some of Ferris Freight's operational funds as it is."

Patris nodded, ignoring the jolt that meant they had left the ground traffic zone. "You'll have to make more than monetary sacrifices. Have you selected the crew of your vessels yet?"

She nodded, glancing through the viewport as she absently ran delicate fingers along the leather seat. Her hand stopped just before reaching his leg, then withdrew. "They will get your herd there quickly and efficiently, but they are no serious investment. Kill them if you require secrecy. I have uploaded their information to the server address you gave me under encryption." The grimace she wore was feigned. She laughed upon seeing Patris's expression. "It's striking how similarly irrelevant my crews and your combat organisms are. Perhaps you could grow me replacements?"

"I could try." Patris massaged his forehead. "Though sentience is an issue. I've never been truly able to replicate that resource." He smirked. "Though, I've never honestly tried. Sentience is irrelevant when I do the high-level thinking for my organisms."

Sybil laughed at that, though she sounded uninterested. She turned and looked hard at Patris. "What comes next won't be easy for you. I bought myself a GDC admiral to command my Void Defense Initiative. You have to give every organism their commands. I read the dossiers on possible side effects of your TCUs. You will be controlling more organisms than has ever been tested. Don't burn out while we are dismantling GDC."

"I created the organisms, and the command device. Don't educate me on the risks. I know them better than you do. I will survive."

"Ensure that you do."

They sat in silence for a time, Patris lost in thoughts of his next war zone command, and Sybil casually staring at him the whole time.

Their transport touched down at the sprawling expanse of Ferris Manor a few minutes later. Sybil and Patris exited their nondescript vehicle. Smiling, Sybil smoothed her gown over her hips, and looked at Patris. "You've never asked me for sex," she said in a pondering tone. "Do you have deviant tastes? You know by now that my sculptor can make me anything I need to be." Her smile faded as her gaze rested upon him. "No, that's not it. Have you relieved yourself of 'base' and animalistic desires? Did you modify yourself?"

"Not as much as you have," Patris replied as the dull gray of his transport touched down. "I still wear the same skin."

Rules

"Why did you replace Martin Ignus as commandant of the Grimvaldi mission, Gabriel?" Isa Ferris asked, not expecting an answer from the man seated before her. A single lamp in the ceiling coughed a putrid light into the cell. Her words hung in the tepid atmosphere. The air was purposefully stale, not that stale air was abnormal in a spacecraft. She had to fight the urge to curl her fingers into fists. Isa crushed the distracting emotion, but not before the prisoner caught a hint of her disgust.

Gabriel gave no response but a hint of a smile curling in his features.

"I understand that you're a war dog. A monster. You're the reason Syndicalists rose up in the first place. Corporate types always say they can use you, but really you just disgust them too." She spoke in a contrived monotone, but venom lurked in her words despite her best efforts.

"Does this tactic ever work, Interrogator?" Gabriel asked, the softness of his words demanding attention.

"Occasionally," she admitted. "But not with your type. The interesting thing about monsters is that you're all proud. I can use whatever tactic I want, but in the end, you'll talk because you want to."

Gabriel put up his hands. "It's a shame that the Ethics Commission is irrelevant. You have grit, but it pleases me to frustrate you."

She sneered, the expression sour. Gabriel was a man of immense proportions. Not vat grown, not clone big, but a simple genetic mishap. Isa knew he thought himself intimidating. Without his battle-harness and his mag-rifle, while her pistol swung at her hip, she found him comical.

"Unfortunately, the empirical evidence disagrees with you." She gestured to the slab walls around them. "You're in a containment cell, after all. An *Ethics Commission* containment cell." She thumbed a switch on the data-band on her wrist. "You took command from Martin on the third winter cycle, as measured on Grimvaldi Prime, did you not?"

"I did."

"Why were you sent to replace him?" she asked, studying his broad-boned hands as he clasped them.

"He failed," he said simply. She could not detect a single jitter of hesitation or spasm of fear. The man was still.

"What exactly did he fail to do? Was it that he failed to defy the Dictates of Incorporated Armaments? You merc types always want the legitimacy that comes from oversight, but when we call, you pretend that you didn't agree to the Dictates in the first place."

Gabriel snorted. The first overt show of emotion Isa had seen from the commandant. "Please," he said. "Even you Commission types know the Dictates are irrelevant. GDC measures operations in terms of success or failure. Martin failed. I succeeded. Don't waste time. Corporate will be here soon, and you'll lose your opportunity to snarl at me."

I can work with this, Isa thought. *He's proud of his record.*

"I am certain Corporate will not view success as creating a publicity storm strong enough to affect share prices," Isa replied. "Is that what they told you? That you're a rising star? Do you have the ear of the Board? You're naive. Your kind are worth exactly as much as they can kill. No more."

Gabriel laughed openly, the mirth ugly when pasted onto his visage. "Be content with the time you have for your preaching, but don't think above your means. It doesn't suit you."

Isa crafted her gaze carefully, coloring her tone and expression with pity. "Oh, you poor, blind man. I pity your misplaced loyalty, Gabriel. GDC treats its employees like a resource, a cheap and expendable one. I can defend you. We can bring the Board down togeth—"

Gabriel cut her off with a slammed fist. The steel table shook, sending a cascade of glimmers off its mirror sheen. "I *am* indispensable. The board came to *me.* You're arrogant. Don't presume what you don't know."

"Prove me wrong then," Isa replied with clenched teeth. "Tell me what happened."

***

Gabriel's boot thudded absently on the steel grate of the chamber, belying his racing thoughts. The chair he occupied was a block of cold ceramic, built for someone much smaller. The climate control suite blinked green on the wall, releasing puffs of new air into the room. The room was sparse to the point of a statement. A perfect setting for torture, interrogation, or orders.

"Martin has failed then?" Gabriel asked, his voice a steely whisper.

"Grimvaldi Prime is to be under your command. We will transfer you all necessary assets and authorities. Expedience is your directive. All else is irrelevant," the man opposite him replied, resting a supple hand on the bare steel table at which they both sat. The man's suit rippled in tailored perfection as he completed the gesture. He was too small for his block of a chair, and looked increasingly uncomfortable with Gabriel's hulking presence.

"Ethics Commission presence?"

"Negligible and irrelevant. You have a month, Commandant. We are on the verge of an embarrassment. Syndicalists do not embarrass us. See to it. We will be watching."

"Grimvaldi is a backwater, barely worth the notation of a colony. Investors don't scrutinize the galactic Periphery."

"When GDC is bogged down in a police action, Grimvaldi will not be hidden by its distance from the Corporate Worlds. The 22nd Foot is yours. Find us a solution, or we will find someone who will."

"It will be done."

***

Isa nodded. "The presence of the 22nd was what drew us here. Such an *infamous* regiment of the GDC foot showing up on the edge of inhabited space was bound to alert us. Have you considered why they sent the 22nd? Seems to me like they were bait, and this operation was your trap. Consider how Corporate can maintain plausible deniability toward any action you've taken. You should reconsider working with us."

Gabriel smirked. "It's not that simple. I can tell you why they gave me the 22nd. I had the audacity to depopulate Grimvaldi Prime, an action that simultaneously spares the GDC a potential embarrassment, and illustrates our willingness to use extreme force. Contrary to your assessment, this action will create a storm of investment from forces with vendettas against the Syndicalists. Even you must admit they have made many enemies. You're wrong, Interrogator: war always has a place, but law does not. The Ethics Commission should know this."

Isa thumbed at the worn horn handle of her pistol for effect, pausing for a long moment while she gritted her teeth.

"Anger?" Gabriel asked while smiling with crooked teeth. "From the Ethics Commission? Interrogator, you're supposed to be the best of us, the force that holds my savagery in check. I pity you. In another world, you and I may have worked together. You've the intelligence to be a commandant. It's a shame that you waste your talents. I—"

"Shut up, shut up!" Isa screamed, her pistol out of the holster, its hovering barrel to the man's chest. The room shuddered slightly. Gabriel's lip curled in an ugly approximation of mirth.

"Shoot, Interrogator."

"Do you expect me to believe that this was a sales tactic? That you didn't enjoy slaughtering Grimvaldi serfs?"

Gabriel smiled then. "One can enjoy one's work."

"Do you?"

***

Task Force Commandant Gabriel Theros wiped grime and sweat off his forehead as he peered at the Olympus Class command Satyr's tactical display, and prepared to commit murder. The five vehicles of the platoon pulsed in blue as they trundled in single file. Wet splats noted the mud jetting from their eight wheels onto the bottoms of their pentagonal hulls.

"Settlement, two kilometers distant. Prepare for contact," Gabriel chimed, his voice turned mechanical by the static of the short-range comms. A chorus of acknowledgments answered in dull affirmatives.* How can a barely armed mob stand up to trained GDC dragoons? *Gabriel thought, flicking an indicator on his display that gave the orders for the other groups of the strike force to engage the Syndicalist forces in the surrounding hills.* It's unacceptable. Martin has failed completely in a war that should have been over months ago.

The Satyr's mag-cannon turrets hummed as their rails were powered. Gabriel checked his own weapon. The mag-rifle hummed in tune with its larger cousins. Gabriel could see the squat box shanties of the settlement in green relief on the display.

"Dismount. Load munitions."

The soft dusting of snow crunched under his boots as he exited the Satyr from its rear ramp. Twenty men of GDC's 22nd Foot followed him, their mag-rifles and boxy canister launchers made ready. Fur-trimmed goatherds with browned skin and crooked village elders stared at the 22nd's overt hostility with wide eyes. A short man, barely reaching Gabriel's sternum, emerged from the onlookers. He was disheveled and hastily dressed at this hour, but the other villagers parted before him. Gabriel raised a gauntleted finger, the scale and plates of his battle-harness clinking softly with the motion.

"Fire."

Canisters and antipersonnel rounds whined from the muzzles of their weapons as the magnetized rails buzzed into life. The short man's face shredded instantly as he took a clutch of shrapnel below his left eye. Coughs of dirty yellow erupted in the crowd as canisters hit home. Gabriel was firing now. His rifle whined and bucked as he put a herdsman down. Those who were not eviscerated in the opening salvo began to scream. No fire was returned. A haze of atomized blood hung over ruptured bodies and exposed meat. The five Satyrs targeted the buildings with their four-kilogram payloads, sending torrents of shattered stone and twisted sheet metal into the air with their furious blows.

"Split and surround, 22nd. Ensure that there will be no survivors. Second company reports that they have engaged with the local Syndicalists. They will return to find ashes."

Within a few minutes, half-scorched survivors began to stumble out of the shattered settlement. Gabriel waved the canister launchers down, and drew a four-foot length of blackened steel. He thumbed an activation switch and the steel hummed softly. He stepped forward to the first survivor; all features and signs of sex had bubbled and charred from its flesh. Avoiding a probing hand licked clean by flame, he slammed the man. The man jerked straight, his flesh hissing anew, and then he crumpled. Beside him, his men were finishing others with the butts of their mag-rifles, or with serrated daggers.

Gabriel wiped crimson on the body of the man. "Mount up. We've more ground to cover. There are fourteen settlements in this valley. They all must burn."

***

"Martin failed because he did not commit the necessary atrocities. I did. I killed what you call 'civilians' because the mission required it. What you don't understand is that there *are* no civilians, just targets," Gabriel said. Isa's revolver trembled as cold scraped along her spine. The room felt claustrophobic despite the ample physical space within. Gabriel stood slowly. The pistol bumped gently against his sternum. "Are you strong enough to kill me, Interrogator?"

"Your confession was recorded." Isa breathed hard. She holstered the pistol in a swift motion. "Thank you for your compliance with the Ethics Commission in exposing this breach of the Dictates of Incorporated Armaments. Your lack of remorse will be taken into account when your trial is held. If you wish to fight these charges, please contact your legal departmen—"

"Listen carefully." Gabriel's voice dropped into glacial cold. "You will give me to the GDC recovery team that has already boarded your ship. Your guards have been killed, and your vessel's electrical functions disabled. Your message never reached headquarters. To any notables, it will seem that the Ethics Commission has overextended its operatives in pursuit of rumor, and been punished by losing an isolated team to Syndicalist raiders. My vessel will have regretfully arrived at your location too late to save you, finding only a shattered wreck."

Isa's pistol once again flew into her palm. Gabriel was prepared. A concussive blow shattered Isa's nose and jaw. The next broke something in her chest. Isa coughed weakly and collapsed as Gabriel snarled and snatched the pistol from her failing grip. He glanced at the weapon, and laughed. Broken manacle chains clinked softly as he moved.

"Idiot. It's not even loaded." He hurled the pistol. The barrel struck her in the eye, and popped it. Gelatinous fluid and blood leaked from the ruptured socket. He knelt, his eager breath sickly warm on her cheek. "I would pity you if you weren't so dense."

Gabriel stood and crushed Isa's neck with a bootheel. The door to the chamber slammed open, revealing two troopers of the 22nd in their standard coal-black battle-harness.

"Corporate wants a status report, Commandant," one said, holding a glass slate buzzing with data. His shoulder plating was crisply stenciled with a lieutenant's chevrons. "Hope I'm not interrupting anything." The man's grin showed in his voice.

"Prepare transport, Solomon. We have no time to lose."

"Aye, Commandant." A gravelly tone announced Lieutenant Argus as the other dragoon.

-Slight delay, local resistance. Grimvaldi mission success, will relocate to Demos for final resolution of Syndicalist threat.- Gabriel typed onto the data-pad, and pressed send.

Gabriel looked at the revolver in his other hand as he sent the message. He wiped eye fluid from the weapon, revealing a glimmer of silver, and the words Last Resort etched on the barrel. He gave a single snort of amusement, and pocketed the weapon as he departed.

Doubt

Sparks fizzled from the bundled cabling on the tunnel ceiling. Gabriel's revolver bucked a slug into the chest of a Syndicalist, the words Last Resort flickering on the side of the barrel. The fléchette round flayed the man's chest, and shattered his ribs. The 22nd pumped canister rounds from their mag-rifles down the corner, their battle-harnesses sprinkled with the blood of their foes. A dragoon with a bulked harness shuffled past, liquid oxygen projector dripping incandescent drool. The corridor roared as a plume of almost-white flame enveloped a machine gun emplacement at the end of the hall. *Corporate equipped us well during the months we traveled to Demos. What do they expect to find here?*

Gabriel slammed a ceramic-steel-clad fist into the crawling and charred shell of a man. His battle-harness assisted the blow and scattered the flaking ash of the man's skull. He detested the slightest slowing of his advance, but he would not leave a man to crawl in the ashes of his dead comrades. A flickering timer on his retinal display reminded him that the limited oxygen supply of his hazard tanks mandated swiftness. *82% remaining.* Gabriel slipped the null-blade from a magnetic clamp at his back, and thumbed it to life. A soft hiss accompanied the motion as the four-foot steel bar atomized dust and soot on contact. He rammed the bar into a Syndicalist. The man's clothing erupted in flame as his skin charred and his blood boiled. The steaming corpse toppled like a sack of liquid.

"Status report," Gabriel barked through the comms.

"West wing secured, Commandant," Lieutenant Solomon Verdax answered in a smooth voice.

"East wing as well, Commandant," Lieutenant Argus Holmarch replied only a moment later.

"Fan out. Argus, take your platoon and block the exits. Solomon, swing north of me. We will flush them into your position, Argus, and you will finish them."

"Yes, Commandant," the lieutenants answered as one.

Gabriel lurched. He glanced down to find the Syndicalist he thought dead with a dagger in his fist. He was still prone, eyes clouded, and likely ruined. *His pain must be immense, and yet he fights on.* Gabriel knelt. The man's boiled skin sloughed off as he moved to strike again. The blow connected. Gabriel grabbed the man's fist, and plucked the dagger away.

He should be dead, Gabriel thought. The man's mouth opened, and leaked blood. Incoherent noises accompanied his struggles. *Impressive. His courage is worth remembering.* Gabriel leveled Last Resort against the man's forehead. The revolver boomed in the tunnel's dead air. Gabriel shook fluid from his gauntlet as he stood.

He gestured forward in a two-fingered point, and his twenty dragoons moved into action. Their boots crunched against the now-baked dirt of the tunnel's floor. The 22nd followed the tunnel as it veered right. Gabriel slid to a stop. A putrid-sweet stench slid through Gabriel's respirator despite the fact that it should have been sealed. The stench seemed to be a medley of a dozen slightly different odors. All of the smells were wrong. They should not be in the tunnel.

The dragoons at Gabriel's side shifted uncomfortably. One man's wracking coughs were audible even through noise dampeners in the 22nd's battle-harness. The dragoons had bunched, attempting to clear their respirators. Gabriel's fist shook angrily as he punched the signal to go forward. The dragoons shook themselves and began to move. Gabriel led, trying to forget the stink that hung in the air with every step.

"Argus, Solomon. Do you smell it?" Gabriel said over the comms.

Argus answered first. "Yes, Commandant, it's not right."

"It's just a smell," Solomon replied, as Gabriel and his men found a heavy iron door blocking the dead end of the tunnel. Gabriel motioned for one dragoon to move forward, and the man produced a taped and wired bundle. "Our hazard suits will shield us from chemical weapons, which is the worst case scenario. It's probably just the stink of their unwashed bodies."

"Don't underestimate the enemy," Gabriel said. "We complete the mission, and that is all."

He brought up his tactical display. The green relief showed that the 22nd had all but choked the tunnel complex. Myriad corridors and chambers had been cleared and marked blue. Only a central dugout remained, and the three platoons had stacked up against the room's three entrances.

"Mark!" Gabriel roared. The bundle, now fastened to the door, flashed crimson and yellow in quick succession. The second stage rent the metal and kicked it inward. Gabriel's null-blade caught the first dazed Syndicalist, a short man fumbling at a clip-fed powder weapon. The man steamed as he became a corpse. Last Resort barked twice and another rebel lost his ribs. A dragoon stepped up, canister rounds coughing from the muzzle of his mag-rifle. In seconds the man had been kicked off his feet, a neat hole bored through his battle-harness. Across the room, an iron catwalk competed with bundles of cabling as a staircase rose to the ceiling. Syndicalists lay prone with mag-rifles of their own. Armor-piercing tungsten spikes burrowed into the earth around Gabriel as the men sighted him. Gabriel threw himself to the earth. Snarls and spits announced the liquid oxygen projector before Gabriel saw the dragoon carrying it stride forward. A gusting roar accompanied the plume of white flame as it engulfed a clutch of Syndicalists blocking the door. Argus and his men stumbled into the breach. The dragoon staggered as the tanks on his back shrieked. The shrieks took on a feverish pitch, liquid spitting out of split metal. The entire chamber was enveloped in flame. Gabriel attempted to shield his respirator but failed. The grill's metal and the polymer of the filter melted together.

Blinded by his failing armor systems, he clawed at the clasps of his helmet. After what seemed like minutes he pulled the ruined husk free. Around him, half a dozen charred dragoons were still. Wails and screams caught his attention, just as the smell of burned flesh filled his nostrils. More dragoons rose, helmets discarded. All the Syndicalists were ash beneath the 22nd's armored boots. Argus stalked toward Gabriel, dust only partially obscuring a mask of scar tissue on Argus's face as he moved up.

"Objective completed," Argus said.

Solomon arrived a step behind, close-cropped coal-black hair revealing a face untouched by battle, with a strong chin only slightly darkened by stubble. Streaks of soot marked the man as having been caught in the blast.

"It's done," Gabriel agreed as he strode toward the blackened staircase.

The hatch at the top of the stairs opened with a shriek of long undisturbed metal. Outside of the tunnel complex, the smell was worse. Gabriel sniffed, and surveyed the survivors. Of sixty, fifty-four had made it to the central chamber. Of fifty-four, forty-six had reached the surface. Gabriel looked to one of the three men who had yet undamaged helmets.

"Trooper Rostam, signal corporate for evac, tell them the mission is complete." The man nodded, and moved his wide bulk away from the rest of the dragoons. Gabriel turned. "22nd! We must carry our dead to the surface. We remember the fallen."

* * *

Even as they worked, servos protesting the strain of dragging dragoons in battle-harness, the stink remained. It caught in the back of Gabriel's throat and refused to move, forcing him to gag ineffectually. With a start, Gabriel almost dropped the body he was helping carry, as he realized the scent was changing. It had an arsenic bite to it now, a bitter burn on his tongue. The dragoon opposite him, holding the corpse by its feet, spat. *He tastes it too,* Gabriel thought. The man looked up. The absence of his helmet revealed a plain face, baked by the sun of a thousand operations on as many worlds. Trooper Paulus gave a short nod. *A good soldier. Volunteers for the worst duties to save his comrades. He'd be dead if I let him take those responsibilities every time he asked.* Together, the two men laid their dead comrade with the other ruptured dragoons.

Gabriel slumped. The foothills of Demos sprawled to either side of the tunnel entrance. Conifers clogged the lower reaches of the hills with invasive vigor, blocking lines of sight as surely as any local flora. Unwittingly, Last Resort was in Gabriel's hands. *Ignorance on her scale is unforgivable,* he almost muttered aloud. *In order to catch the prey, their cover must be burned. We did what was necessary for the mission to succeed, and to minimize the 22nd's losses. We are the 22nd. That is our role.* Yet he could feel the flesh and bone of her neck cave under his bootheel, even these months later. *Curse her for making me kill her.*

Gabriel drew in a breath. An acrid taste coated his tongue. He spat. With a wave of his arm, he summoned Argus and Solomon. The two men arrived—Argus with his ever-present scowl and Solomon with his easy smile.

"It's even worse outside the tunnel complex," Argus replied to the unasked question. "The mission did not require chemical scanners, so we don't have any. Even if it did, we likely wouldn't have been issued them."

"They're just a pack of Peripherals. They were using gunpowder weapons," Solomon said. "The 22nd was hardly required for this."

"We sent a message," Gabriel said coldly. "Corporate wanted these Syndicalists eviscerated. We did so. That is our role."

"Commandant," Argus asked. "What about this mission could not have been done with an incendiary device?"

"Certainty. This way we know no one escapes before the consolidation crew arrives," Solomon said simply.

"No one in an underground complex survives burning the oxygen out of it," Argus said.

"It was a propaganda piece," Gabriel replied. "If dragoons massacre the last resistance on this planet, then it's clear to the shareholders and those who contracted us that GDC cares about the success of the mission deeply enough to send important operatives. Bombs can kill, but they do not provide the emotional weight of boots on the ground. It is a regrettable necessity."

Argus grumbled, and pointed to the dead. "Corporate's message was worth their lives?"

"Not ours to decide. We simply kill and die where we're ordered to," Gabriel answered. "Morality is impossible to determine from the ground. War is emotion. Decisions are reason, and reason is scarce when bullets begin to fly. I'd prefer a better struggle, but this is better than none at all."

"Your philosophy," Solomon began, "Is impossible. Corporate would love it if we were machines, but we are not. We think, we feel, and there is nothing that can stop that. Following orders isn't an excuse."

"Then why are you here, Solomon?" Gabriel asked.

"I'm here because I—" Solomon's answer was cut short by a dull crack as his skull ruptured. Gabriel blinked hot crimson moisture from his eyes as he jerked backward. Dull pings and thuds chattered. Around him, dragoons were leveling mag-rifles to fire at scuttling targets hugging the tree line further down the slope. The smell thickened, acid coating Gabriel's tongue. He reached for Last Resort's holster, only to find the pistol missing. Cursing, he stooped to wipe cerebrospinal fluid and blood from Solomon's mag-rifle, the handle slippery even with the assistance of his battle-harness.

"22nd!" Gabriel snapped a pair of solid rounds down toward the tree line. "Form a perimeter. Conserve ammunition. Rostam, status on evac?"

"Unknown, Commandant," Rostam replied. "22nd channels are down hailing 13th and 5th."

"Word on the 6th, Jager?" Gabriel grimaced as a solid hit bent his torso plating. The projectile survived contact, landing on the needle-covered earth beside him. A pallid barb, far too organic in nature for Gabriel's comfort.

"None."

The projectiles stopped. The scuttling silhouettes melted back into the forest as abruptly as they had arrived. Five more bodies lay still within the dragoon's hasty semicircle, including Solomon's skull-less body. Gabriel knelt to inspect the dead, noting that each fallen had been killed like Solomon, helmet-less heads ruptured. The smell had changed, earthy and sweet, enough to make Gabriel heave.

"What was that?" Paulus asked in a gasping breath, his harness pitted and littered with dents.

"Darwin," Gabriel replied venomously, holding a barbed spike of pearlescent white in his fist. "Darwin Bio-Security."

Power

Sybil aerated her wine with a casual whirl of her wrist. The deep sapphire liquid left a thin band of color on the wide glass. Her hair hung like a cloak of midnight around her bare olive shoulders. She wore her hips wide, with liberally sculpted curves.

"The vintage is excellent. I'll have to place an order for a reserve myself." Helen wore a snowy gown, and reclined in a leather chaise opposite Sybil. "I'm glad we can visit more often. I missed how close we were in childhood." The choked light of the Fiscal City filtered through a series of amplifiers to light the garden with daylight.

"Finest wine I've tasted," Sybil mused. She sipped casually as she studied the other woman with innocent glances. *Your restorative treatments aren't up to Fiscal City Standards, Helen. I can see the hint of fatigue around your eyes.* "Are you enjoying your return to the Core?"

"The Core has its charms," Helen admitted, "but so do the Peripheral Worlds. When was the last time you saw a real forest? Have you ever seen one?"

"Only in exploratory streams," Sybil replied. "They bore me." She flicked a hand, and a servant appeared, carrying two more glasses.

Talk stretched for two hours and nineteen minutes as Sybil watched while the additive in Helen's wine drain her thoughts and actions of any logic or foresight. The woman laughed heartily at nothing, and shed tears at the slightest provocation. *Oh Helen, your time in the Periphery has dulled your wits. I cannot have pity for someone who does not use a taster.* Sybil grinned. Patris had replaced the annoyance of a follower with the convenience of a poison sniffing micro-organ mounted on her olfactory lobe.

"I hope you give GDC what they deserve." Helen chattered, eyes glazed slightly.

"I will, but we must speak privately. Order your servants not to interrupt us. I have already done so. We cannot take risks with what I must tell you."

Helen nodded vigorously, and fiddled with a data-band on her wrist. Sybil waited to see that it was done, and sealed the room with a few touches of her own data-band. *All the additive needs to fully activate is a hormonal rush.* Sybil stood, and allowed her gait to accentuate her sculpted features. Helen gasped. Sybil watched the additive flood Helen's brain with chemicals. Sybil met the woman standing, and laced her fingers through Helen's hair. She pushed the woman down on the leather chaise, and tore off her dress. *Now, Helen. I take your company and your dignity.* Sybil's face contorted in a smirk, and she began to indulge herself.

They lay intertwined for a long minute. Sybil casually monitored the effects of the additive on Helen's psyche. *It's time to pay for your weakness.*

"Helen," Sybil said as she caressed the woman lightly. "I need something from you."

"Oh, anything." Helen raised herself on a crooked elbow and looked intently at Sybil.

"I need Alloy Industrial."

Helen balked, even through the chemical haze. *Stronger willed than I thought, but too trusting for that to matter.* Sybil leaned over and kissed her lightly on the neck. Helen drew in breath sharply, and nodded.

"I don't understand why, but I don't think I can refuse you anything."

"I know." Sybil pressed a fingertip on Helen's lips. "I need your company. I need you. Please, I can't do this without your help."

Helen pulled back, and fiddled with her data-band. "What will happen to me?"

"I will protect you, you've always wanted me to."

"It's done." Helen blinked slowly, a confused look crossing her face. "I can still cancel, I don't know why that seems important."

It's wearing off.

"It isn't."

***

Helen followed Sybil in a borrowed dress, brows consistently furrowed. Sybil couldn't keep the grin off her features. Helen glanced at her worriedly.

"Sybil. What's going on? Where are my clothes? Why is my account manager trying so desperately to contact me?" Helen's voice was frantic, her eyes wide.

Sybil savored her fear, and then answered.

"Do you remember when you told me that you weren't prepared to look after the White dynasty?"

"Yes." Helen missed a step.

"I worried for you," Sybil replied, "But I found a solution."

"I don't understand."

"I didn't expect you to, but allow me to explain." Their path took them through doors and marble and granite hallways. "I was dishonest. I need your company, but I don't need you, or your family. So I drugged you, and since you trusted me, I now own your company. The White family has no holdings, and the Ferris family continues to grow."

Helen stopped dead in her tracks. "What? How?" She felt at her dress, memories coming to her in spurts. "No. No, Sybil, I can't believe you would—"

"You've always been trusting. That is your *greatest* weakness." Sybil shook her head softly, and reached for Helen's shoulder. The woman gave a strangled wail, and recoiled. Sybil grabbed her anyway. "It will be easier for you, starving to death. Or if you would prefer, I do require escorts. I can offer you a decently paid position, but I warn you some of my clients have odd tastes. I can—"

Helen screamed. She clawed at Sybil's arm, and drew blood in furrows on her perfect skin. Footsteps rang in the hall as Helen knocked Sybil over in a fit of rage. Sybil gave a gurgling laugh through a broken nose. Two massive security guards in charcoal suits lifted the flailing Helen off of Sybil, who rose and spat blood on the front of Helen's dress.

"Thank you for your assistance, Helen. History may not remember you, but I will." The security guards turned and dragged Helen away as she finally sagged, defeated.

Pain

Mottled light whispered through the needle canopy of the multitudinous conifers of Demos. The 22nd stalked in a loose pack of interlocking zones of fire and hissing servos. Acrid notes hung in the back of Gabriel's throat as he coughed to dislodge them. Solomon's unfinished sentence echoed in Gabriel's head as he walked, the motion jarring his thoughts as much as his flesh. His brain functioned on armor stimulants alone. *Forty-five hours, and six ambushes.* Beside him, Paulus gripped his mag-rifle with white knuckles. Groans accompanied his movements, and his arming coat was visible through gaps in armor plating, or through places where pieces were missing altogether. Other dragoons, the thirty of the company still alive, had disheveled suits and open wounds, souvenirs from ambushes encountered earlier.

Gabriel's bandoliers bounced almost empty, just as he knew the rest of the company's did. Scabs from a host of tiny wounds pricked at the jagged edges of sheared armor plates as they scraped against his skin. Dirt and grime filled wounds and left them aching as he walked. He did not groan. *We will die here,* some part of him mumbled in the deep recesses of his mind.

"Commandant," Paulus said, arm outstretched and offering a canteen. Gabriel shook his head, the motion hard due to his leaden muscles.

"Pass it along."

Paulus nodded, and moved away.

Rostam clunked up from a stand of trees to Gabriel's left. The comms trooper's squat frame would have been above average height anywhere else, but in the 22nd, he only reached Gabriel's shoulder.

"Commandant," he said, his dull monotone seeming oddly out

of place to Gabriel. "Corporate's not responding. 13th and 5th were ambushed as well, and took heavy losses. Only the 6th Jagers seemed to escape; they were in air transit at the time of Darwin's attack."

"Situation?"

"Fucked, Commandant," Rostam said, without a hint of emotion. They both grinned.

"Regroup the 22nd and all other forces on Ironback Pass. We'll form a base of operations and attempt triage."

Rostam nodded. "Permission to speak freely, Commandant?"

Fucked wasn't speaking freely? Gabriel wondered. Rostam seemed to take Gabriel's pause as a yes, and spoke.

"If Corporate's dead—and they are—you're in command. Do you plan on fighting Darwin on the ground?"

"If we can."

"You know we can't, Commandant. We're battered and broken, and we have no idea how many creatures Darwin brought in."

"You're right," Gabriel said. "But if they're here, we have to assume they also have stellar superiority, otherwise our fleet would have maintained contact. We're alone until we can be relieved."

"We're going to die here," Rostam blurted.

"If we do, they will die with us," Gabriel replied.

Rostam laughed.

"Who, the nonsentient war creatures that can be grown in vats? Why does it matter?"

"No. Their commanders are human. I met one at the GDC Expo a year ago. Sniveling lunatic never stopped complaining about a buzz in the back of his head. It may cost us, but if we can't get off this rock, then we'll ensure the least of their worries is a buzzing head."

Rostam nodded his helmeted head.

"I guess it's the best revenge we can hope for."

"Corporate will come." Gabriel gripped the man's warped shoulder plating. "There's too much of an investment here for them to waste. They have to."

"I hope you're right," Rostam replied.

The man left, disappearing into a swaying copse. Gabriel coughed again, trying to clear the phlegm from his throat. He vomited instead. Last Resort's empty holster clattered softly on the armor of his hip. Dark blood smeared the tooled leather. Fatigue assaulted him, and his vision began to blur. The trees around him blended softly; his eyes narrowed gradually. His feet were lead, but he pushed onward.

***

Gabriel sat at a mess hall table with a steel mug of coffee in his hands. The transport vessel was well lit, clean, and full of smiling servants. Gabriel shifted uncomfortably. These fatigues are too light, too soft. Gabriel's hand fell softly on Last Resort, buckled in a leather holster on his hip. He grimaced, and shook his head.

A shot broke the mundane chatter. Screams and shouts echoed through short hallways. Gabriel was on his feet, scanning the room with Last Resort. Another shot, metallic this time. Mag-rifle, *Gabriel thought. He burst into a whitewashed hallway, and saw Solomon holstering his mag-rifle as he towered over a disemboweled rating still weakly clutching a gunpowder pistol. The man was a husk. Gabriel was unsure whether it was from age or just working conditions. He watched the man leak onto the pale surface for a long moment, and looked to Solomon.*

"Syndicalist sympathizer," the man answered. "Shot Dommel while he was shitting."

"Did he say anything?"

"The usual. Said he had the moral right to own the means of production, said the workers should rule the workplace. I finished him before he could."

Gabriel gave a short nod. He fought the urge to crush the man's skull. Dommel was a good dragoon. Reliable, if uncompromising. Said he was paying for medical treatments for his wife the only way he knew how. Syndicalist scum.

"Sympathizer?" Argus's harsh voice asked. Solomon nodded. "I'll never understand why they fight."

"Really? Have you ever been to an ice mine on Demos? Or seen the slaves on Serenity's Well? It's not really that hard to understand why they want out," Solomon replied.

"I understand wanting out. I don't understanding picking a losing battle. Fighting GDC is suicide. If you're willing to fight, then do so for GDC, and survive."

"It's not about survival to them. It's about change."

"Pointless. Dead is dead."

"You don't understand," Gabriel added. "Their lives are a losing battle. To a Syndicalist, fighting is no different than

working. Either way he dies."

Argus snorted. "But they have courage, a marketable asset that could be used to get them all out of the losing battle, and yet they don't use it. Wasted potential."

"Isn't being a dragoon a losing battle as well?" Solomon asked, and pointed further down the hallway. "Dommel was careful. He checked his lanes of fire, always maintained his gear, and modified his harness. He died. What's the difference?"

"We have a chance. We have a navy," Argus said as he spat.

"They have a reason to fight!" Solomon slammed a fist against the bulkhead. "What stake do we have in the conflicts we fight in?"

"We are dragoons," Gabriel replied. "Why do we fight? We have something to prove. Every operation is a chance to prove our merit in a crucible. We don't inherit wealth and family name like a Ferris, or a White. All the glory we get is because we fought for it. What is a better reason to fight than to show that you're worth something? To really prove it. Why does the GDC matter? Look at the history of our combat operations. You can watch us lead the 22nd to victory. Wealth doesn't do that. True merit is only paid for in blood."

"I don't understand how that motivates you. No one knows your name outside GDC. Maybe even no one in Corporate. Who are you proving this to?"

***

Gabriel awoke and stopped. Grasping vines shimmered as they choked the trunks and branches of conifers as far as he could see. Even rows of needle spines and follicles covered the twisted mass. Gabriel's fist shot up, clenched in warning. The dull rustle of dragoons stopped immediately. He signed Paulus and Argus over.

"Commandant," they answered.

"Darwin biotech." Gabriel pointed his finger, the gnarled plating disturbing the light. "Call up dragoons who have combat machetes, or hand axes. We'll have to cut our way through." The men nodded, and stalked in the direction of other clumps of the 22nd. Gabriel approached the gleaming net cautiously. His finger-plate clinked softly upon contact with a vine, and soft snaps told him dozens of hairs had broken against the ceramic-steel composite. A gust of wind caught the spines, and they chattered and rustled in reply.

Eight men in varying states of disrepair drew up with blades gleaming. Paulus was among them, a two-foot blade with a wicked forward curve smirking in his fist. Gabriel nodded, and pulled his null-blade from its sheath. He thumbed it to full power, and smacked the vine. A hiss and pop greeted him as the ionized steel jolted the vines, but they didn't move.

"It's metal," Gabriel said with a grunt.

"Dragoons, cut," Paulus called. A chorus of shearing scrapes and bestial grunts accompanied their work. Their armor-assisted blows cleaved gaping rents in the mass. Sickly pus revealed a plantlike interior as they cut. Gabriel felt the smell catch at the back of his throat. He doubled over in wracking coughs.

The strip was only three meters deep. Red welt lines marked the dragoon's exposed flesh as they moved back into position. Gabriel's mind wandered. *Solomon was about to say why he was here,* Gabriel realized. *He's dead. I can't ever know why one of my best officers wanted to be a dragoon.*

"What's on your mind, Commandant?" Argus asked as he approached.

"Solomon," Gabriel replied. "He always criticized the dragoons. Why did he join? Why did he make a career in a field he despised?"

"I'm sure he had a good reason." Argus's gravelly tones spat the words more than said them. "He never did anything he really didn't want to do."

Gabriel nodded, and felt Solomon's brain-splatter moisten his cheek again.

"Normally that would be a cause for reprimand." He rotated a sore arm, pushing cracked armor and ignoring the pain. "But in his case, it was why I promoted him. He wouldn't care that I was a commandant. He'd say shit was shit when he saw it."

"He saw a lot of shit. Little bastard never stopped complaining." A smile died on Argus's lips. Gabriel's too. The ground ascended before them. Boulders stippled the undergrowth and decaying pine needles, tripping the occasional weary dragoon. Scattered logs, some newly severed and others sagging with decay, provided the illusion of cover on the uphill rise.

"Still no contact with Corporate?" Argus asked.

"No. Comms are dead. We have to assume that Darwin has somehow developed naval craft, or allied with another of our rivals."

"So it's a coup?"

"That's what I can't understand." Gabriel clenched a fist. "There are no competitors. GDC invited Darwin to the Expo for a buyout. We have a monopoly on force, save for the Syndicalists."

"Those bastards barely qualify as an insurgency." Argus's laugh sounded in a stony clatter. "At best they're a reason to leave behind shit rotations. I'd rather be in the mud than on parade detail again."

Gabriel grinned. "They're a convenient way for Corporate to justify protection costs. That's as good a reason as we need to make planetfall."

Argus slammed a fist against his ruined cuirass. "Hammer and anvil. It's the 22nd's way."

Ahead, two dragoons loomed over the scrawny Jager in sweat-ruined fatigues. Gabriel had to remind himself that the man would have looked average in another setting, but beside the 22nd he looked adolescent. Chevrons of rank and the man's familiar hawkish features labeled him Colonel Doran Felix of the 6th Jager corps.

"Commandant," Felix said with an easy grin. "How are Corporate's poster boys?"

"Worse for the wear. Where were your men when Darwin hit? Ironing their parade uniforms?" Gabriel replied.

"I figured if we looked better, we might get more airtime." Felix shrugged. "Now I'm almost as stained as you."

"Almost," Gabriel agreed. "How did you get here before the 5th? They were much closer when I contacted them."

"I 'requisitioned' a contingent of Satyrs from the ammunition depot we were supposed to be defending when we heard of the attack. I packed it up and brought it with me. We would have flown straight to Ironback Pass, but our transports got lit up by a pack of air superiority fighters with VDI stenciled on them before we could board. We rode on the Satyrs and brought the ammo while hugging the damn forest so we couldn't be targeted."

"Good work. We're almost dry. Do you have any armor repair kits? Or any intel on what VDI is?"

"No, and no. Corporate must not have been expecting a protracted engagement. I have water at least, and some ration packs, but not much else."

Gabriel nodded and scraped a hand over his scalp. His gut groaned, and he forced it down.

"I'll take my platoon and walk the rest of the way," Felix said. "The 22nd deserves a rest."

"We're barely combat capable," Gabriel agreed. "Send the Satyrs to resupply and pick up the rest of the 22nd. Rendezvous at the former Syndicalist earthworks at the top of the ridge."

"Aye, Commandant." Felix saluted.

"I need you to be my eyes. Operational command should be from space, but our operational has been sunk," Gabriel said. *This mission is shit. We can't achieve the primary directive without stellar support. Besides, fighting Darwin isn't a contest of merit, it's surviving a storm. There is no chance to prove anything here.*

"Understood. I'll keep the 6th mounted and mobile. We have contact with elements of the 3rd armored brigade; I'll transfer them to the ridge. It looks bad."

"It is. We have no air support, and I have to command from the ground. We have no intel on the size, disposition, or even genetics of the enemy. Our forces are scattered, understrength, and we have an ammunition reserve designed for surgical strikes and not a protracted battle."

"What do you do when you know you're going to die?" Argus rumbled.

"Fight anyway." The three men answered as one.

***

The Satyr's interior chattered as it trundled across the rough terrain. Small data displays fizzed uselessly as they tried to connect to a corporate intelligence network. Paulus was opposite Gabriel, hunched over his combat blade, trying to work the ruined edge back into something semi-usable. He had been at it for hours. They reached the strong-point forty-nine hours and six ambushes after they cleared the Syndicalist earthworks. The hatch opened to reveal a slice of night poisoned by void-craft engines. Gabriel rose.

The earthwork's haphazard weave of slit trenches and rifle pits was rent and sundered. Skeletal remains of pillboxes and machine gun nests cut a dismal profile on the ridge top. Gabriel's feet sucked into mud with every step he took. Further along the ridge, other Satyrs disgorged clumps of men. A curse cut the air. Gabriel spun and saw a dragoon on his knees, clenching battered fists and mauling at his combat helm. Another scream spun Gabriel, and another man writhed.

"Contact!" Gabriel slammed into cover behind the Satyr shoulder first. Paulus was beside him in an instant, mag-rifle humming in anticipation. Gabriel's eyes darted to the downed dragoon as another scream echoed from further along the ridgeline. The downed man had patches of exposed skin raked in weeping red welt lines. Gabriel snapped his gaze to the other man squirming in mud. His welt lines throbbed. *Darwin fucking Bio-Security. Even the plants fight.*

"False alarm, stand down," Gabriel called as he turned to Paulus. The man dropped hard, armor squealing in protest. Two more screams sounded. Paulus groaned at first, sweat beading the man's brow in an instant.

"C-commandant?" The man stuttered as his face bloomed red. Then he screamed. The man's voice was gone in an instant. His battle-harness clunked against the Satyr's hull intermittently. Gabriel looked at the man's weeping wounds, and loaded a fresh clip from his bandolier. He cycled to canister rounds with a flick of his thumb, and leveled the muzzle. Gabriel clenched the trigger, and Paulus was shredded from the neck up.

Gabriel turned to the next dragoon, and ruptured him with a pair of shots. He cycled to solid rounds with another flick, and shouldered the weapon. The last dragoon managed to nod his thanks through the agony, his voice stolen by pain. Gabriel sighted the man's head, and finished him.

The mag-rifle slipped from Gabriel's fingers and stuck quivering in the mud. Last Resort*'s* empty holster smirked through the dragoon blood that splattered it.

Limits

Patris Telby reeled under the assault of mundane stimuli on his sensory organs. The landing craft's engines popped softly as the dull gray metal cooled. The buzz thickened into a throb as his booted feet sunk softly into the loamy earth. The sun was just past the horizon, and it bled too much light for his eyes as he walked. Sybil's garb was odd. Patris had never seen her outside of the silks and velvets of the Fiscal City. She wore a plain but cupping sundress of cream that offset her seemingly natural bronzed skin. Her blonde hair was topped by a wide-brimmed straw hat. She smiled, but the expression belied her worry.

"Headaches?"

"Worse this time. I'm not used to the sun. Or the smell of the grass." She laughed.

"Try sleeping more. Or just running simulations less."

Patris leveled a stare.

"And have substandard organisms? I think not. GDC dragoons are harder to kill than Syndicalists."

"You need to be alive to command them as well." Sybil rested a hand on Patris's shoulder. "You may have subordinates, but they are not sufficient for our goals."

"I know my limits," Patris said, grinning through his head pain. "I'm nowhere near them."

"Let's work, then," Sybil replied, and Patris began walking again. The pain subsided, but remained. The clearing rose into broadleaved grass plants that formed an impenetrable mass of green. Snorts and snickers marked the four combat bipeds that took guarding position around the pair. *Marcus controls them well. He's the only Conductor who has come this far. He will be an asset for what is to come.*

The trail descended to reveal a rich, crop-carpeted valley with a whitewashed manor that sprung wings into a courtyard of lush, ovular gardens. A crisp-suited man with sun-darkened features strode the path to meet Patris and Sybil.

"Welcome to Serenity's Well. Master Stewart has been expecting you."

The interior of the manor was dark oak and carved baseboard. The furniture had opulent but rustic leather upholstery. Geoffrey Stewart reclined and accepted a short glass of amber scotch. Patris lifted his glass to his lips, tasting the flavor and feeling a slight burn near his sternum as the liquid was purged of alcohol content and potential poisons by one of his newer organs.

"Your creatures are impressive. It's been a few years since I've had the time or inclination to leave my planet. Do you command them remotely now?" Geoffrey asked.

"Darwin has made many advances in recent years. That's why I'm here."

"I already have a GDC contract for terrestrial security. Theirs comes with a package discount to protect my shipping. Your products look special, but I'm sure they aren't as cheap."

"I need biomass in quantities large enough to increase the operational sizes of my herds exponentially," Patris said.

Geoffrey smiled, and laced his fingers after setting down his drink on a cherry side table.

"That I can provide." He motioned, and a servant appeared with a data-slate displaying production ledgers. "I have a marginal surplus, perhaps four or five million tons that could be allocated to your account."

"I need more, and I need cheaper. Tell me, how much does GDC charge for their protection?"

"Monopolistic rates," Geoffrey admitted. "I don't see an alternative. You can't provide naval support."

"That problem can be temporary, if you help me." Patris leaned in. "There is a very real possibility of breaking the GDC's monopoly on force. It is in your interest to assist me."

Sybil cast a sidelong glance at Patris, and gave an almost imperceptible raise of the eyebrow.

"No, it is not. Even if what you say is true, my planet is stationary. If I switch security providers, I am a target; in fact, I am a priority target because my elimination would provide ample warning to any who would follow in my footsteps."

"We will have the element of surprise. We can stun the shareholders with a few battles and force a price drop."

"That's an assumption, Patris, and you know it. I've seen the GDC fight. They sent the 6th Jager to put down a Syndicalist enclave just thirty miles south of here. They massacred them. Not a single survivor. Your creatures are impressive, but they are not convincing."

"My combat organisms are empirically cheaper and more effective," Patris said with a snarl. The buzz was roaring in his head again, and a bead of sweat glistened lightly on his forehead.

"What Patris is trying to say—" Sybil began in a warm and friendly tone,

"—is that it's not an assumption. It's the most plausible outcome," Patris finished.

"I understand that, but I can't help you blindly. I'll sell what I can, and forget this conversation, because I hope you win. But I can't risk my holdings."

"That's all we can ask." Sybil rested a hand on Patris's leg gently, but her fingers began to clench firmly. "We'd best take our leave. Thank you for your hospitality. Hopefully our business will allow us to reach the Periphery more often." She stood and dragged Patris with her.

***

"What was that?" Sybil said, whirling on Patris as their landing craft's door closed. Patris sighed despite himself. *The light on this planet is absurdly bright. Is the star here more potent than the sun?* Sybil continued. "You alienated him almost immediately. You said you could achieve preferential pricing for biomass, and this is your plan?" She looked at him, then her posture softened. She moved to him, and ran her hand along his arm.

"He resisted more than I had anticipated," Patris replied.

"Of course he did!" She sighed, exasperated. "It isn't advisable to reduce your profit margin for questionable gain. They're all going to resist, Patris, because they hold power in the status quo. You need to convince them that the gain justifies the risk."

"It isn't a significant risk. We're going to win."

"You know we can't prove that."

"It's true, Sybil."

"Irrelevant, Patris. Perception of truth is more significant than objective truth. Especially when manipulating. No one but you understands how far Darwin has come, or what capabilities you have."

"I know that," Patris replied, fists clenching. "Intimidation is also a tactic. You undermined my certainty."

"What exactly is your next move?"

"I land combat organisms. I make a show of force, and renegotiate." *It won't be much of an operation, but it will be something to burn this isolationist's manor.*

"You know that would alert GDC to our plans and presence. I want to see Stewart humbled as much as you, but it has to be silent."

"Don't lecture me on tactics. I understand the risk, but I need the biomass. I share your concerns, but I don't see another option."

Sybil shook her head. "This is my arena. Let me do my work."

Patris stopped for a long time.

"I'll give you three days. Then I land my herd."

"Be ready to depart. Deployment will not be necessary."

***

Patris and Sybil reclined on a pair of leather-upholstered chairs bolted to the decking of their transport. Wall-mounted screens displayed Serenity's Well as it faded into the suffocating blackness of space. Patris could feel the buzz invading his concentration. Pain provided an ever-present companion to his thoughts. He grimaced and Sybil noticed.

"What did you give him?"

"Geoffrey is an easy man to understand." Sybil grinned. "I gave him what none of his slaves could: a partner who appeared to enjoy his advances. He was rather malleable after that."

"That's it? He seemed more strong-willed than that."

"I have my methods, Patris." Sybil rested a hand on Patris's arm. "It's a shame you won't let me show you them."

"I have simulations to run." Patris massaged the front of his head as they cut through the void.

Mettle

The boy shuffled his feet as he peered over the scores of nervous men in the line. His feet ached. The concrete was too hard; his soles were too soft. The dead air was tepid, and too silent for anywhere else in the Fiscal City. Above and ahead, two men stood tall and proud in battle-harness. Their heads scanned the crowd diligently as a suited man recorded names on a slate in his hand.

Behind the boy, the mob of noteworthies was visible in their finery through a space between two monolithic obsidian bank towers. The line moved, and he moved with it. Some fled before they reached the end. They were weak. The obsidian towers paled to opacity, revealing hundreds of drone-like workers in various states of boredom. The boy smiled. He shifted, readjusting his tattered pants with dirt-speckled hands. He would prove them wrong. He would show the galaxy what he was worth.

A cold fist gripped his innards as a voice cackled faintly somewhere inside the recesses of his mind. He gulped, and fought himself back into control. He stepped forward.

"Name?"

"Never had one."

"Alley-born? Irrelevant. Your origins mean nothing to the dragoons. I need a blood sample." The man extended a thin needle toward the boy's bared wrist. The man smiled when he looked at his slate. "Your genetics are suitable. You are now Gabriel Theros, recruit of GDC, candidate for the 22nd." Gabriel smiled and wiped the spot of blood as it appeared on his skin.

"Thank you."

***

Blood welled around Gabriel's fingers. He recoiled, and the fluid clung to him. A man writhed below him, screeching and clutching feebly at his stomach. Gabriel remembered the blade in his hands. It glinted, grinning through the crimson.

"Again, dragoon. He isn't dead." Gabriel couldn't place the voice, but he obeyed. His arm jolted as the tip of the blade caught before slipping through the man's ribs. The squirming stopped.

"Not clean, but dead is dead." Gabriel stood, and the knife dropped from his fingers. Blood trailed from his fingertips as the weapon fell.

"Never drop your weapon." A blow toppled Gabriel, and his face landed in the man's ruined belly. Iron coated his tongue.

"You don't understand yet. Another."

***

"I hear they modify the 22nd," the woman half-yelled over the formless noise that was supposed to be music. Gabriel nodded and shifted his titanic shoulders as he leaned against the seamless brick wall. People walked and jittered aimlessly around them in time to the noise. The woman ran delicate fingers through waves of chestnut hair. She grinned.

"What all do they modify?"

"Whatever they feel useful for combat."

She pouted slightly in response. "Nothing more ... fun?"

"No," Gabriel replied. "Sorry to disappoint."

"Oh, you don't." She smiled, and pulled close.

Gabriel eyed her openly.

"If you want to see a modified human, I'm on leave. I have another few days." Gabriel's broad features broke into a grin. "I also have a hotel room outside the barracks. It's ... secluded."

The woman seemed about to respond when the noise died. A scratchy voice replaced it.

"Leave is canceled, 22nd. Report to Commandant Velman for assignment."

Gabriel straightened and smiled.

"Change of plans," he said, and cut his way easily through the crowd.

***

The Interrogator loomed over him. Her slender hands rested coolly on her hips, one hand softly grasping Last Resort's handle in its holster.

"Are you proud of what you are?" she asked, moving slowly closer.

"I am."

"Why? What have you done of merit? You kill for someone's profit, and the galaxy is worse for it. I'd like to think they conditioned you. I'm sure they did. But you're a different case, aren't you? The 22nd are no standard dragoons. You enjoy this."

"What I do is real, Interrogator. I fight in an age of complacent inherited wealth. You're worse. You attempt to be just when everyone is indifferent to justice. If I'm a fool, you're insane."

"We're the same, Gabriel. We both fight for lost causes. I for justice, you for merit. We are both doomed."

"That's true," Gabriel admitted. "I didn't want to kill you. You have to believe me. I respected you more than anyone else outside the 22nd. You had merit."

"I know. You had a sort of justice to you. A warrior's code, both idiotic and admirable. You're the only honorable psychopath I ever met."

"I gave an account of my life. Give me one of yours. I read your bio after I killed you. You are a Ferris, someone of old wealth. Why did you leave your sister the empire and join the Ethics Commission?"

"My wealth was meaningless. How many palaces does one family need? How many worlds can you own before buying another becomes irrelevant? My family has enough money that they could sit still for a century. Money was pointless."

"Why the Ethics Commission? You cannot compete with wealth by advocating for weakness."

"We need limits. Without them, we ignore sense and turn towards comfort and away from duty. The Ethics Commission reminds the Fiscal City of how their lives cost others. But you killed me."

"You gave me no choice, Interrogator."

"I know." She paused. Her features were blurred, as if they were about to come in focus. Gabriel strained to remember her face. Elegant, high cheekbones and a steel set to her jaw. "You are right, Gabriel. This will not change without violence. You acted as you thought necessary. I stood in your way, and you needed to move forward. But you fight for nothing more than respect. You fight for the status quo, not against it."

"I am on the wrong side." Gabriel finished her thought.
"You are."
"It's too late now, Interrogator. GDC is falling, only to be
replaced by something worse: Darwin."
"Why do you hate them? Don't their Conductors show strategic
brilliance?"
"They do, but fighting beasts is not war, it's survival. Without
war, you cannot be brave. Without bravery, you cannot show
merit. You can only survive. It's not the same."
*   She walked closer, and drew Last Resort. "I think you need this*
more than I do." She proffered the weapon, butt first. Gabriel
reached out, and clasped it.
"I hope I see you again, Interrogator."
"You won't. Fight well, Gabriel." She blurred, then dissipated.

* * *

Gabriel awoke. The ceramic of his plating beaded with condensation as he rose in the predawn gray. Beside him, various pentagonal hulls thrummed softly, engines cycled quiet. It was more a comfort to attempt some level of stealth than an operational advantage. Gabriel had no illusions. He knew that Darwin could smell *exactly* where they were. He knocked on the hull of the vehicle he was beside, and the rear hatch banged open to reveal Rostam in his decrepit harness. The man gave a short nod, and Gabriel entered and sank into an empty command suite. *What I wouldn't give to be in orbit, properly commanding this battle. Or to have shuttles that we could evacuate with.* Gabriel glanced at the largest display.

Sixty-one thousand, three hundred and fourteen dragoons and Jagers silently sighted their mag-rifles, and ensured they had cycled to solid shot. Fog choked visibility in soft morning light. Four thousand, six hundred and ninety-three Satyr variants supported the battle line's entrenched position. Embedded in the reserve trenches like hull-down beetles, Tartarus mobile mortars cycled their launchers into readiness. Held in clumps like predatory felines, Gorgon gun carrier crews completed last checks on the temperamental ten-kilogram mag-cannon that replaced the standard carrying capacity. Invisible bubbles of security centered around clusters of Centaur flak tracks as their quad-barreled canister launchers darted attentively to target potential threats.

Gabriel's armored bulk contested with a dozen input nodes and data-choked screens as he squatted inside an Olympus command vehicle. Amber indicators flashed for every GDC position on the ridgeline. Ammunition and casualty warnings gave estimates of critical mission failure that burned in his vision. Rostam's fingers flew across communications consoles opposite him. His deadpan tone gave orders too complicated to be transmitted automatically as Gabriel formulated the battle plan. Infrared data streamed the heralds of their defeat in a white-hot mass clawing its way around their entire position. The air filter of the Satyr was robust, enough to filter oxygen out of toxic air on a dead world. The smell was weakened, but not defeated.

"Why don't they just glass us from orbit?" Rostam asked, in between relaying fire solutions for Tartarus emplacements.

"Shareholders," Gabriel replied while flicking reinforcement orders for the 6th Jagers. "A ground battle is visceral. It puts their dominance in clearer perspective for corporate video streams. I'm certain that's why they let us regroup."

"Then we're dead anyway?" Rostam said, a hint of despair touching his voice.

"We were dead when Darwin ambushed us outside the tunnel network, Rostam. Nothing we do will change that."

Rostam nodded. "But we fight anyway."

He opened a view of lumbering heat signatures, and alerted a pack of Gorgons. The air vibrated in an instant. Crimson runes denoted flight packs of VDI ground attack craft as they began bombardment. *They're identical to GDC patterns. Flying wing design, prow lasers, stealth.* Gabriel grimaced. Aircraft cleared swathes of fog with incandescent contrails as they stitched the ground with canister detonations. Some GDC runes darkened crimson. The Centaur battery surrounding the Olympus command vehicle spun to life.

The vehicle toppled. Gabriel's skull punched through the main screen. Burnt electronics assaulted his sinuses in acrid notes. Rostam scrambled to his side, knocking loose an input node. Gabriel pushed the ruined display off himself as he tried to stand. Together they slammed armored shoulders against the back hatch, and wrenched it open.

The air buzzed with exchanging fire. Columns of ink belched from shucked pentagonal hulls, as the surviving vehicles hurled their anger skyward. Their Olympus was splayed drunkenly on its side, the remains of a VDI aircraft pinning it to the ground. Gabriel unclasped Solomon's mag-rifle from his back and cycled it to solid shot. *We're already blind. We needed that vehicle.* Rostam righted himself, wiping blood from a scalp wound out of his eyes. Scattered clumps of Jagers held in reserve painted crimson puddles. Gabriel almost tripped over a charred half-ribcage as he began walking. *Their assault force will already be moving. We need to reinforce the front with antitank weapons. The Gorgon's Ten-K mag-cannons are the best we can hope for.*

"We need to get those Gorgons in position," Gabriel shouted over the dead-wash of battle noise. Somehow Rostam understood that he should follow. Gabriel forced his muscles into motion and ignored the chafe of his harness. Shrapnel screeched over his head as a nearby Centaur was immolated by a lance of stark white. Fire bloomed to the other side of him, and a wall of hot air kicked him off his feet, and tumbled him into a crater. Mud sucked at his pauldrons as he rose.

The air was suddenly clear of VDI ships. Distant roars noted the line had made contact, and staccato booms issued intermittently from the remaining Centaurs.

"Rostam!" Gabriel screamed. The man scanned shattered debris, oblivious. *Shit.* Gabriel's legs found motion. He skidded in front of Rostam, and the man's eyes found his.

"Commandant, are you hurt?" The man's voice boomed in Gabriel's ears.

"Your eardrums are ruptured, trooper," Gabriel said, exaggerating the words.

"Shit," Rostam agreed, attempting to moderate his volume, and failing. Gabriel motioned to follow, and began to run. He skidded over a burned hull and leaped a depression, feeling pain sink into his muscles. Mortars wailed overhead, signaling distant detonations.

Dragoon bodies lay scattered across the mud. Gabriel stooped to tear a helmet off a corpse. He wiped blood from the interior, and failed to completely clean it. He slammed it on anyway, and activated the comms.

"Felix, report."

"Heavy assault, two-pronged. Must be hundreds of thousands of them. Permission to reinforce on the flats? The enemy will have less cover there, and my Satyrs will have more room to maneuver."

"Granted. Be ready to hit and run, you are the hammer."

"Damn it, Gabriel, do you want to be spent by Corporate?"

"I'm already dead. You don't have to die with me. Besides, you're easier to hide than we are."

"Affirmative, Commandant. Try not to have your death recorded for the shareholders," Felix replied. Gabriel cut the link and ran. Rostam thundered behind him, silent in his fury.

"Gabriel to the 22nd. We are the anvil. Regroup around the 5th and prepare to weather the storm. Bring in as many Gorgons as you can get, we'll need them."

As a chorus of affirmatives guaranteed the eight thousand and twenty-nine remaining 22nd would comply, Gabriel saw his target. Thirty Gorgons hummed as their massive cannon snouts searched the horizon for targets. His harness clanked on the hull of a Gorgon as he scaled it. The hatch popped open to reveal a stained face.

"Drive. We reinforce the 5th." The man hesitated before finally making out the rank chevrons on Gabriel's stained armor. Rostam slammed home a second later, and climbed atop the vehicle. Blood and mud speckled the hull wherever they moved, arms flailing to get a handhold. The Gorgons lurched and bucked over crater scars.

The air was baked dry by jet contrails. Plumes of jet spun lazily into the air from a hundred different fires. Five gargantuan shelled creatures lumbered at the front of Darwin's advance on the 5th. Thousands of scuttling bipeds spat projectiles from their arm mounts as they hid behind thick bone-shields that replaced their off hands. Gabriel rolled off the Gorgon just as it fired; the shockwave flattened him before he could duck. One of the monsters opened its scaly maw, and vomited clear liquid that billowed into white gas on contact with the air. Dragoons screamed wetly, and died. Massive tungsten slugs tore gaping rents in the creature, gouts of hot blood pouring from gaping wounds. One beast crumpled.

Gabriel was up, ignoring the fire being traded above him. He cycled to canister and his mag-rifle roared. A swarm of chitinous bipeds slammed barbed shield edges into the exposed flesh of a pair of the 5th. One lurched sideways in a spray of burgundy, hunks of chitin clattering against the nearby carapace. Rostam added his fire, kneeling in the lip of a small rifle pit.

The 22nd arrived in three wedges, spitting incessant death from the mouths of their mag-rifles. Argus strode at the tip of one and gave Gabriel a helmeted nod. The Gorgons poured fire into another beast, toppling it. The creature shrieked down the ridgeline, crushing bipeds like locusts under its bulk. Howls announced VDI strike craft. Canisters erupted in the 22nd's loose wedges, shredding fully armored dragoons. Nearby Centaurs answered, and ruptured a pair of attack craft as they peeled off.

The air went dead. Gabriel picked himself off the ground he didn't know that he had fallen to, and spat out the aftertaste of the smell. The 22nd took their places in rifle pits and trench lines, scavenging the remains of dead dragoons for ammunition, and piling their bodies for makeshift parapets. Gabriel slid into a rifle pit beside Argus and Rostam.

"Solomon would probably say Corporate abandoned us," Argus said.

"He'd be right."

Argus nodded, and jerked a thumb toward the sky. "We won't last long against that."

"We'll make one or two more strafing runs, maybe more," Gabriel agreed. "If Darwin doesn't kill us first."

Argus tore his helmet off. His eyes glowed with fury. "Then why the hell are we here? Why the hell are we sitting on a damn ridge that exposes us to enemy fire?"

"No tunnel network would save us either. The best we can do is show the shareholders that GDC battle deployments have tenacity. Show that we can't be replaced by beasts."

"They're winning!" Argus roared. "Why the fuck does it matter if we show honor? We're dead!"

"What do you want me to say?" Gabriel replied. "Corporate doesn't give a shit about us? That we're assets?" Gabriel felt Solomon's death-spray on his cheek again, watched Paulus writhing in silent, unrelenting pain. His voice broke. "Even if we're GDC's best asset, we're still an asset. Expendable. That's what being a dragoon means. There's honor in it, a fatalistic honor. But there is no scenario where we survive."

"Commandant—" Argus began.

"I know. It doesn't matter. Darwin has more here than either of us could have imagined." Gabriel stood and flicked on his regimental comms feed.

"Gabriel to the 22nd. Darwin has already achieved victory. Any action we take here will be hollow. I have only one viable solution. We stay. We are the anvil. Felix is the hammer. He will smash a hole in the encircling forces for the remainder of the 13th and 6th Jagers. They will scatter and look for any form of civilian transport. We can hope their fleet element is not significant enough for full blockade. I will not order this, 22nd. I ask it."

"What about Corporate?" A soft voice asked. *Elsa Olbricht, captain, 22nd Dragoons.*

"They have abandoned us. We have become too cost intensive to recover." Affirmatives met Gabriel's plea. Beside him, Argus's granite countenance gave its assent.

"This is it, 22nd. Here we have a chance to show that merit comes from sweat and steel, not from wealth or family name. We are here because we are the ones with courage enough to face the storm of inhumanity that assails us. Ancient cultures used to live for this kind of war. A good death, an honorable one. We are the last warriors, men and women of true merit. Thank you, 22nd, it was an honor. I wouldn't die alongside anyone else." Gabriel cut comms, and found Felix.

"Commandant!" the man answered breathlessly, "My Satyrs are ready. We're hammer. Where's the enemy?"

"Link up with 13th. Punch through the encirclement. Scatter. Get off world."

"I—"

"Not optional. Get out. We'll hold them here." The link died for a moment.

"Affirmative, Commandant," Felix replied at last. "It was an honor."

"It was." Gabriel tore his helmet off. The smell assaulted him, but he breathed deeply. He could taste his death on that air, and not for the first time, fear clenched a fist in his guts. He clapped a hand onto Argus's shoulder.

"If they're going to bomb us, let's make sure they hit themselves as well."

Argus grinned, red- rimmed eyes framed by blood-clotted dirt. "Commandant," he replied. "I'm willing to die with you."

"Thank you. That's where we're going."

Rostam, noticing something was decided, thumbed his mag-rifle to life and nodded. Gabriel and Argus did the same.

The 22nd emerged from cover as the rest of the GDC forces melted away behind them. Their disheveled harnesses lent failing protection as they formed a loose wedge. Rostam's grim face covered Gabriel's left, and Argus's steady fist covered Gabriel's right. They crested the ridge, clambering through trenches and foxholes, knocking aside fallen comrades, and marking their names. They cycled to canister in unison. Gabriel breathed.

Below, Darwin was already reforming. Massive creatures strode upward, packs of bipeds avoiding their footfalls. The smell was solid in the air. Around Gabriel, men vomited. Wings of VDI craft screeched overhead. Dozens, maybe hundreds. Gabriel adjusted his bandolier. The enemy host reacted as one. Bipeds interlocked shields. Shadows materialized on the 22nd's flanks, feline shaped, eyes of amber. Bulkier, top-heavy bipeds formed blocks behind the shield wall, baying in the dead air.

"Forward, 22nd. We fight the storm." They charged. Thundering footfalls accompanied the barks of their mag-rifles.

Gabriel's clip went dry. He loaded another. The shield-wall buckled. The three hulking macro-tortoises vomited. Dragoons scattered, their rapidly corroding bodies hissing, their formation dissipating. Here and there, heavy-weapon-toting dragoons took aim at the hulking creatures. Rostam took a barb under the chin, and he toppled. Gabriel sidestepped, and heard a dozen projectiles plink off his armor. Solomon's mag-rifle bucked in his fist. Blood ran from a nostril as his sinuses balked at the stench. Gabriel shucked two more bipeds and slammed a new clip home.

Last Resort's holster smacked against his armored hip, pitted and scarred from glancing barbs. Gabriel cracked through the skull of a biped with his fist, drenching his entire arm in blood. He grabbed a mass of wet tissue, and hurled it in the eyes of the next approaching biped. The creature squealed, and was replaced by three others. Argus opened them.

A feline dove through the opening. Gabriel was on his back, knocked aside by Argus. He stood stone still, with his chin raised. The scaled beast snarled a grin, and rent Argus apart with a massive blow. Solomon's mag-rifle put the creature down.

Two more felines rolled into the gap. Gabriel lost feeling in his legs as they were snatched in the jaws of one beast. Pain immolated his nerves, and snapped out. The other circled, gobbets of saliva dribbling on Gabriel's exposed face. Gabriel felt Last Resort's holster finally break off. Solomon grinned above him, flanked by the firm stances of Paulus and Rostam. Argus raised his arm in salute.

Well, Interrogator. Gabriel sighed. *Now we both die for nothing.*

Wrath

Patris welcomed the needle of stimulants. Ice soothed the ache in the back of his skull and behind his eyes as the chemical sleep replacement flooded through his veins, but a dull buzz remained. The white-frocked woman holding the needle stood and checked a glass slate coruscating with the data of his vitals. She nodded. A gust of scentless air filled Patris's nostrils as Sybil entered the sterile chamber from a reinforced door. The mottled gray cut of her dress contrasted with the bleached surroundings. She wore her hair in spun gold, bound and resting over the bronzed skin of a bare shoulder. Eyes of emerald narrowed in concern as she entered.

"You need to sleep before you command ." She stood before him now, hands resting on her hips.

"There are too many simulations to run, too many combat organisms to test." The room shuddered slightly. Sybil's head turned to look at the observation console by the door. "It's nothing," Patris said. "We'll have to deflect the occasional asteroid when hiding in a belt of them."

"I understand," she replied. "GDC Naval superiority is close to unchallenged. I need to be sure that we're ready."

"That's why I can't stop running simulations. Even now I can't stop thinking about the next creature I have to test. But there is nothing that my concern will do. *The Recompense* outguns any GDC craft currently in existence, and there are nine of her class in total. Our fleet is larger and better equipped in this region, and they don't know we're coming." Patris sighed. "But you're right. I can't help thinking we missed something."

"I'm confident we didn't."

Patris nodded. A smirk caught at the edge of his lips. "This will be the largest war since the Alien Contact War centuries ago. To think we are about to end such a long age of useless peace."

Sybil grinned in response, the gesture revealing pearlescent perfection. She shuffled slightly, and reached out to Patris with a soft hand.

"We're unstoppable."

Patris laughed.

Sybil flinched almost imperceptibly, but continued. "Once we win here, we will be the most powerful force in human history."

Patris nodded, feeling the buzz returning. Even now, he could almost taste the rush of command. *Soon I command the largest herd I've ever assembled against a determined and disciplined foe. No longer am I confined to Syndicalists and inconsequentials. It begins today.* He looked up to see Sybil's mouth half-open in mid-sentence. She stopped, brows creasing slightly.

"Are you sure about the boarding action? We can delay a few hours, give you some sleep."

"I'm ready. I will do this."

"I don't doubt you," she said softly, "but I need you for what is to come. Don't waste yourself."

Patris grunted, and shook his head.

"Well," Sybil continued, her voice forcibly purged of worry. "We have time, let's make use of the comforts I had installed." She led Patris to the door, and through a small hallway. The sitting room they entered was the perfect temperature, and scentless, as Patris preferred.

Patris sank into a velvet-upholstered chaise as he reclined alongside Sybil. On a short table beside him, dry sapphire wine sat in a crystal goblet. He picked it up and swirled it. The pain was back. Subtle this time, it throbbed behind his eyes, at the base of his skull, and inexorably moved down his forehead. Now the pain stampeded, snarled, and faded again. Patris hissed almost imperceptibly. *The compound didn't work. No matter. When I command, the pain disappears.*

"Something wrong?" Sybil asked, casually taking a draw from her own glass, reclining on an identical chaise.

"Why bother changing your appearance? We're in space. There is no one to impress."

"You're wrong. Besides, the longer I keep one appearance, the harder it is to sculpt away. It's excruciating if I leave it longer than a couple of months." Her words hit him, but they took a long second to batter through a new wave of pain. She looked at him again, longer this time. "Are you sure it's time to strike? You're visibly ill."

"I'm fine. My TCU malfunctioned during a simulation yesterday. I'm not used to spending so much time away from my work."

She nodded, but the gesture lacked any understanding.

"Is it salvageable?"

"It's temporary. It will be finished with enough time for me to run the last preliminary tests and get the herd to operational standards."

"We only have one chance at this. I've attracted more unwanted attention and made more enemies in the past few months than I have in the past ten years. It's exhilarating, but it's unsustainable. I can't set up for another attack. If we act now, it has to work."

"It will."

"I know," she said with a sigh. In two more sips, she had drained her glass, and a manicured and suited servant filled it anew. Phantom combat organisms clustered around the periphery of Patris's vision. The creatures capered, beckoning. He wanted to stand, but Sybil's sudden touch kept him in his seat.

"If centuries of noncompetition have made GDC complacent, how will we avoid the same fate? They fought efficiently during the early colonial period when they were contracted by the nation states. They drove off the aliens and exterminated them when no one else, not even the titanic nations of Earth, could. Their sense of superiority is earned."

"I don't know if we can," Patris replied, suppressing a grimace of pain. "It is too much to hope that our power will last forever. An ancient general once said that glory is fleeting, but obscurity is forever."

"A wise man, if deluded. Generals served the state. They allowed themselves to be exploited."

"Not this one. He usurped power, and turned the nation upon his neighbors. He did what his contemporaries thought impossible, before finally being brought to heel by a coalition of almost every major power of his time."

"It surprises me that the nations did not expect what GDC would do. If military men rebelled before, why would they not again? By contracting GDC, government sealed its own fate."

"They were the greatest fools," Patris agreed. "They didn't

realize how quickly their international law and sovereignty would
break down when faced with overwhelming force."

"Not unlike GDC now. They think the shareholders in the Fiscal
City have the same tolerance for risk and violence they had
centuries ago." Sybil laughed. "When was the last time any
shareholder has ever been *really* at risk? Ownership is
concentrated too far from the brutality of the Periphery to
understand reality. They have had power too long to appreciate the
severity of our challenge."

"We will be no different. We will have our time, and then we
will die like our predecessors."

"But this time we'll be alive to face them."

"If I can make it so, yes."

Sybil reclined again, letting out a small sigh. She sipped wine
for a long second before she spoke once more. "I'm not used to
this."

"War is different. In time, you may come to prefer it. I do."

"No. War is different, but I meant this. Us. I'm not used to
having an equal."

"Neither am I," Patris replied. The pain had settled some, but
the phantom organisms now cavorted in the center of his vision,
snarling, snapping. They beckoned him on with clawed
appendages before loping away. They reappeared, and repeated
their call.

"Why is it that you're the only man I've ever wanted, and the
only one I can't have?"

Patris blinked, and took too long to respond.

"I'm not trying to manipulate you. I don't think I could," she
continued, reaching a hand out toward him. A macro-tortoise faded
through the wall, and belched corrosive fluid. Gas billowed into
the room as the searing liquid jetted toward Sybil. Patris leaped up,
and pulled Sybil from her chaise. She started, but looked around
intently. The macro-tortoise faded, becoming spectral before
finally dissipating.

"I thought I saw—"

"Patris?" Sybil's voice wavered slightly.

"It's nothing." Patris looked at Sybil, and ignored the snapping
maws that seemed to threaten her. The smell of her was
intoxicating, as he was sure she wanted it to be. It dulled the
intermittent jolts of pain in his skull. He blinked, words dissolving

in his mouth as he attempted to spit them out.

"I mean this. Your will is impressive, you resist my advances because you know I'm testing you. You passed. We're more than allies, we're akin."

"You're right, I—"

The comms console near the door chimed out the end of Patris's sentence, noting that the remainder of the fleet had arrived.

"Ferris Freight Void Defense Initiative assembled. Formation assumed and ready for combat action." The voice was sweet, the phonemes assembled from the most calming female source available. Patris raised an eyebrow at the choice as he stared into Sybil's emerald eyes.

"Trying to replicate the warmth of a mother's voice? Are you that nervous?"

Sybil shrugged. "Once we've scattered GDC before us, shall we celebrate?"

"What did you have in mind?" Patris asked, grinning as he moved toward the door.

"I was thinking I should improvise, just to see what it feels like."

***

Sybil sat at the rear of *The Recompense*'s bridge, arms crossed tightly with a jittery anxiety. Before her, dozens of men and women sat wired into consoles, their veins flooded with hormones and stimulants to calm nerves and heighten brain activity. A bulked man with the sword and crosshairs of the GDC logo inked in his neck, and the chevrons of an admiral on his shoulder, sat on a raised central throne, giving orders in a regulated voice.

"Begin."

Ferris Freight's Void Defense Initiative clung in a pack to a screen of asteroids just out of scanning range of the long-range detector suites of GDC's largest dry-dock facility: the Thusis Shipyards. VDI's long-range scanners, built to out-range those of this exact facility, washed over their target while Sybil watched the main observation screen as it displayed the enemy deployment. The installation was gargantuan, larger than many asteroids in the nearby belt, and studded on every one of its twenty triangular faces with ships in various stages of production and repair. Light bloomed against girder sections as sheets of armor were fixed in place. Gaseous expulsions snorted from venting ports across the dock's surface as spacecraft were pressurized and given oxygen from vast reserve tanks in the internal workings of the shipyard. Around the writhing mass of industry, the thirty enemy craft—only two of battleship displacement—and a dozen cruisers hung lazily, scanning with keel-mounted cannons.

Fifty ships, the entirety of the VDI, skittered into place. Most of the smaller vessels were of GDC specifications, bringing identical guns to bear on their targets. Nine Isa Class battleships hung behind the screen of smaller craft, their diamond slanted hulls and pyramidal prows studded with a dozen primary cannons in bulbous multirotational turrets. Other small guns dotted the hull like lines of rivets, scanning with micro-lasers for incoming debris or suitable targets. The matte exterior of its layered armor drank the light from the fleet's engine blooms.

Thusis went dark. *The e-security team has done their work.* Sybil breathed hard. *Now, we begin.* The station's protocols rebooted, but the picket had noticed. Maneuvering jets flared instantly in the GDC Fleet.

The VDI screen emerged from the asteroid belt in a volley, unleashing glittering red beams from their small cannons. Fire stitched along the length of four GDC cruisers as their oxygen bled into space. One, shuddering with the force of secondary detonations, rent apart in a spray of bent plating. Nearby ships jumped into action in an attempt to avoid collateral damage. The VDI's screen parted, revealing the disfigured silhouettes of Isa Class battleships as each of their twelve macro-lasers targeted a small ship. Stark white beams gutted destroyers with contemptuous ease. Keel beams from GDC craft responded, detonating the fission reactor of a VDI cruiser and sending its spinning bulk through a clutch of three destroyers. The smaller craft crumpled beneath the onslaught, detonating them and spreading a rumbling chain of havoc and devastation within the tightly packed formation.

Two GDC cruisers sighted *The Recompense* and snarled their defiance in laser form. The shots connected solidly on the prow of *The Recompense*. Sybil was on the floor as the ship shuddered, blood pooling around her nose. A nearby rating, face bloodied by his fall, picked her up.

"First layer has taken the brunt of the damage. Elasticity remains on the outer shell," a man's voice called, his tone chemical serenity.

"Return fire. Priority targets: battleships," the admiral stated. On the view screen, green runes noted affirmatives from the captains. Growling shudders accompanied the resighting of the turrets, followed by a shriek as they all fired at once. Their target weathered the blow on its prow; claw-like rents marked with brief blurts of smoldering fire glinted in the void. From a second angle, the guns of *Marauder* slammed into the craft's unprotected flanks, venting writhing specks of humanity into the vacuum. On the opposite side of the picket, GDC's other capital ship returned fire, its keel beam scoring a direct hit on the engine pods of *Scorn's Promise*. A blue bloom of plasma tore the craft apart from stern to prow as the Isa Class battleship's oversized reactor went critical.

"Admiral Martin Ignus to all Isa Class cruisers," the bulked man said. "Ensue prow facing to priority targets. Cruisers, find your GDC counterparts and immolate them. Ground team, stand by for boarding protocols."

A lethal lattice of energy connected the two fleets with pinpoint precision. GDC craft slunk in and out of cover behind the listing wrecks of their comrades, letting the corpse craft take pummeling hits. Their cover disintegrated slowly as the wrecks were atomized under concentrated fire. On the main view screen, an estimated casualty ratio blinked green: *12.2% | 88.5% Imminent VDI victory.*

"Cyber attack on my mark," Admiral Ignus droned.

"Now it's up to you, Patris," Sybil said, laughing through the pain of her shattered nose.

***

The deck beneath his borrowed feet thundered, and the darkness jittered. Adrenaline capered through Patris's veins, and the buzz that had been invading the back of his skull was mercifully gone. He swapped from team to team so fast he vomited, but he didn't care. *This will be my finest hour. Let my lieutenants terrorize the 22nd. I will cripple the company.*

Twenty thousand organisms, the maximum command capacity of the Darwin Mark III Tactical Command Unit, twitched in nervous response to his euphoria. The new creature he had designed for this mission made up the highest percentage possible given the lack of the central birthing vats. It cut a hulky and short silhouette, tungsten-reinforced scales covering its broad bipedal form. Its hands were clawed and four fingered, with forearms

enlarged for crushing. Beside the stomach was a miniaturized
version of the macro-tortoise's acid gland. A muscle-wrapped tube
traveled through the creature's neck and allowed for a belching
acidic vomit. Thunder boomed in the drums of Patris's borrowed
ears, and the darkness died as the boarding craft's hatch opened.

Mag-fire burst half a dozen combat bipeds as the dragoons
holding the breach opened up. Immolating gouts of white caught
organisms in bulk and roasted them in their reinforced shells.
Patris's new assault bipeds filled the breach with caustic bile,
wrenching screams from the throats of the defenders. An assault
biped screeched, and dove over the corpses of its fellows to sink
metallic claws through a dragoon's faceplate. The man's skull
disintegrated under the wrenching claws of the organism. Patris
switched. The Thusis shipyards bled fire from twenty breaching
wounds, each releasing a thousand deadly organisms into the heart
of the facility. Patris switched. Here, a pack of fifty-four assault
bipeds rushed a corridor, bathing the GDC dragoons in acidic
liquid. The sizzling armor almost drowned out their shuddering
screams as they cooked on the floor.

Panic spread. The corridors were studded with doors marked in
numerals. *Bunks?* Patris shrugged off the thought, and spiked the
creatures' rage. They howled, and began tearing at hinges. Patris
switched, monitoring overall combat now, flooding undefended
corridors with shrieking creatures for a flank in the two hundred
and twenty-third deck. On the upper decks, he bypassed heavy
resistance, leaving a pack of combat bipeds to tie up the defenders
before encircling them for the kill. The entirety of the GDC 8th
Dragoons was deployed within the halls of Thusis, and their ten-
thousand-strong garrison was faltering. Patris switched.

Adrenaline pounded through his muscles so hard he twitched.
His mind soared. A chorus of almost twenty thousand bayed with
delight at his commands. Patris switched, his expanded mind
cataloging combat fatalities with ease while he guided a pack of
combat organisms to the fight. Patris switched.

The dragoons shattered. They dropped mag-rifles that glinted
with chromium polish. Patris spurred a combat biped onward, and
slammed its shield into the fleeing man's back. He crumpled and
skidded with a metallic wail as his harness sparked along the
grated floor. Patris shoved the creature's projectile arm under the
man's helmet, and felt the creature's endorphins as his own when

the barb cracked through a plastic eye lens and sprayed crimson on a clean wall.

Patris switched. He cannoned an assault biped's arm through the wailing frame of a white-frocked man, tearing a clutch of vertebrae from the man's spinal column. Patris switched, watching indicators feed his certainty that GDC was in full rout. Patris switched. His synapses sung with stimulation as he ordered hundreds of organisms individually. Their footfalls resounded in his veins as Darwin's braying monsters performed a cacophony of violence. Patris switched, watching a dragoon choke on pheromone stink as a combat biped took aim. He switched. Casualty data blurred his vision, cost estimations seared through his head. A scream escaped his real lips, then laughter.

***

Sybil heard a man's wail faintly from the bridge. She ignored it. *Victory Achieved* blinked in green on the main viewing screen. The crew cheered as the chemical calm dissipated and their true emotions returned. Sybil gave a shuddering breath, then smiled.

"Begin streaming. "

Veins

Patris. A discombobulated voice slithered into Patris's thoughts. The buzz was thunder. It hammered each thought as it tried to surface. *Patris.* The voice was familiar, gentle, with a cadence of folded steel. *Patris.* He woke.

A cold blend of blood and vomit filled his lungs as he tried to breathe. He coughed the mix up as he tried to breathe again. Harsh lights lanced his eyes, reflecting off pale walls. Rotary hammers revolved inside his skull. The smell of evacuated bowels met his nostrils, and he heaved a dry stomach.

"Patris!" Sybil cried, the skin of her hands spattered with his blood-flecked bile. She screamed something as she knelt beside him. He tried to see more, but the light was too much, and his eyes closed. A prick of pain accompanied liquid warmth in his veins as his muscles relaxed, and he collapsed.

***

Sybil's calm drained away as the GDC fleet drew closer. Block orange numerals gave the command deck an iridescent backlighting. *I'm reading into this,* she snapped at herself. The time ticked slowly overhead. *Twenty-seven hours until GDC fleet elements reinforce.*

Sybil caught the arm of a passing rating. "Find my personnel, and get the Acquisition room ready."

"Aye, madame," the woman replied, and hurried off.

A small section of the view screen buzzed with Patris's spiking life signs. A video stream showed him quivering under piled sheets, heaving ineffectually on an empty stomach. *You idiot*, she almost cried aloud. *Didn't you check on test subjects for adverse effects? It looks like you're a chem-fiend post-overdose. You're too driven. More driven even than I am, I think. You'll have to forgive me for tasking your scientists on a cure, but I need you.*

Sybil produced a small slate from her dress and thumbed it on.

The Galactic Stock Exchange took center stage. GDC stock pulsed red, noting a drop of 30% over the two days Darwin and VDI victories had been broadcast publicly to every major hedge fund in the galactic Core. Darwin's price blinked green, almost doubled. Ferris Freight was subdued, but had seen growth nonetheless. *Darwin has more available capital than I do, and Patris can't give me access to it.* She stalked from the room, with a grin curving her lips.

Patris's chief accountant was a weathered alabaster statue of a man, his pale features warped by wrinkles that increased as he constantly furrowed his brow over Darwin's accounts. The room that had been given over to Darwin's financial services glowed gray with bulky utilitarian computing banks.

"Arthur," she said, running a finger playfully along her lip. "Would you be able to assist me, I'm in terrible need of your help."

The man stared at her blankly for a second, then returned his gaze to a screen choking on data.

"What is it? I'm allocating funds. We took greater losses than predicted on Demos, so I need to increase the operational budget slightly." The man's voice gave no hint of any change in his demeanor. Sybil scanned him with modified eyes, and read no increase in heart rate. *Of course.* She repressed a laugh at herself. *Patris knows me. He had his staff modified for this exact reason.* She smiled slightly despite herself. *I could use him now.*

"I need Darwin's capital," Sybil said, posture snapping straight. "Konrad will look weak. I can convince the board to supplant him and end this. Why waste unnecessary funds?"

Arthur's thinning eyebrow raised. "I'll need confirmation from Patris, I—"

"He's comatose. I need the money now. We merged, remember? I have the ability to transfer funds, and I need them now."

"The merger contract also included a payment. I haven't received it yet," Arthur replied, flicking to the accounts tab.

"It's coming. Even the Fiscal City can only process so many transactions. Patris and I talked about this. Did he not inform you?"

"He did, madame."

"Then it's *my* capital also, is it not?" Sybil stretched out a hand.

"Allow my acquisition team to utilize your resources, and we win this war. I see no negative outcome from this action for either of our parties in any scenario. If GDC's board refuses, and they will not, use your funds to requisition more assets."

Arthur nodded.

***

Sybil's acquisition war room was a panoramic enclosure of screens and input nodes. Lights welcomed her entrance, and a dozen reports were brought forward as she entered. Her fingers danced across fingerprint scanners that emerged from a wall. Her face cracked into a predatory grin. She pricked her finger to unlock the last layer of security to her accounts. Her grin split open further as she began buying GDC stock in droves, taking advantage of the chaos and shaken investor confidence that her recent victories had brought. *We don't even need to sink the GDC fleet to defeat it. We just need to buy our way in. GDC stock has become extremely affordable of late,* she thought, making the necessary investments.

Sybil switched to the Fiscal City market logs, watching her name rise higher and higher on the list of GDC shareholders. She slipped past Konrad after liquidating her stock in Alloy Industrial. Data buzzed on newsfeeds, idle chatter becoming frantic as Sybil snapped up stock suddenly jumping in price. *13%.* She almost salivated with anticipation. *The GDC board of directors now primarily represents my interests. They should contact me in minutes.*

It was sooner than minutes. A chime notified Sybil of an incoming communication. She accepted it, pushing down her glee, and steeling her features. Lukas, a weathered man of perhaps fifty, reclined in a slate suit, eyes darkened by fatigue.

"Ferris," he said with a sigh. "You're clever, but what exactly is the point of this?"

"Lukas. I've no time or inclination to play coy. I am now the single largest shareholder of GDC, and I have demands."

"What exactly makes you think that I have any inclination to listen to you?" Lukas asked with a snarl.

"You have no choice. You represent my interests now that I'm a shareholder, and I will express them. You've seen exactly how far I'm willing to go in order to further my goals. Remove Konrad as CEO. I've just made a public spectacle of him. GDC may still save face if this debacle is blamed on him and not the shortcomings inherent in GDC's products that I have so vividly illustrated in these last few days."

"You engineered a war just to unseat Konrad? What did he do to you?"

"Nothing. That's not my only demand. I will be Konrad's replacement. GDC's operations will be my prerogative."

"Why the fuck would I give you control of the company you just humiliated?"

"You gave the reason yourself. I defeated GDC with limited and comparably small resources. I'm better than Konrad. I slaughtered his precious 22nd. I captured his shipyards. Do you need more evidence that I'm a better candidate than he is?"

"You also caused a 30% drop in our net worth. What you've done proves only hostility."

"How else could I expose the fragility of GDC from the outside? Before I humiliated GDC, no one would have believed that there were any challengers to its monopoly. Now it's evident that GDC no longer has the best products on the market. I do."

"Why capture GDC then? Why not tear it apart?"

"Please." Sybil couldn't repress a sneer. "Why fight when the war is already won? I could continue to tear your company apart piece by piece, but I'd rather take my prize while it's still intact. The less damage I cause to GDC the better off you and I both are. I gain a legitimate company and you don't lose all of the value in our stock."

Lukas laughed. "I don't think your position is as good as you claim. I think this is desperation. I think you're trying to bluff your way into a monopoly. I'm not Helen White. The board will not stand for your empty threats."

Sybil's predatory grin only widened.

"Let me make this perfectly clear, this is not a negotiation. I do not *need* GDC. I *want* it. If I cannot have GDC I will incinerate it piece by piece until all you own is ash. I will scupper your fleets, slaughter your armies, and then I will move on Earth. Nothing will be spared my wrath. I will kill investors. I will enact martial law and enforce it with hulking abominations that walk the streets under my command. It will be a tale of hell come to life for the express purpose of your demise. You will submit to my will or be added to the pile of bodies I have climbed to be where I am. Do you understand?"

Lukas swallowed, but otherwise maintained his composure. "This communication is over."

The stream died. Sybil chuckled. She found her data-slate on a low table beside an ancient vintage of burgundy wine. She motioned a servant to pour her a glass as her fingers met the slate. She selected the payments tab and selected the Darwin payment. *Set status: Delayed indefinitely.* Her fingers shook ever so slightly. *This way, we win.*

She moved into the command deck again, swirling wine as she walked. *If the board doesn't take me seriously,* she mused, *I'll give them an incentive.*

"Obliterate Thusis. Send it to the board, and depart outside of GDC search protocols," she called. "The sight of GDC's prize dockyard being obliterated will convince them of my sincerity."

Her bought admiral grinned even through the emotion suppressants.

"Aye, madame," he said, and lit the void with VDI fire.

***

His senses tried to grasp any stimulus. They failed. Words faded into sound that dissipated slowly to noise. His muddled wits latched on to a clear voice, crisp with command but tempered by concern. *They agreed.* He tried to process the data. His brain was liquid. The thoughts slid through. A warm touch blossomed on the skin of his cheek. *We won, Patris.* He thought he understood, but didn't know why it mattered. The buzz was returning.

He screamed.

www.ingramcontent.com/pod-product-compliance
Lightning Source LLC
Chambersburg PA
CBHW020542130626
46552CB00007B/2724